"You kn... querida, never say never"

His sideways glance caught her heaving bosom. "You gave every appearance of enjoying yourself when you kissed me." Her response had delighted him.

"That was not a kiss."

"It was not?"

Megan chewed fretfully at her full lip and stared stubbornly out the window. "It was... a reflex," she retorted in a driven voice.

"Indeed? I can only say that you have the best...*reflexes* of any woman I have ever come across."

Though lacking much authentic Welsh blood, **KIM LAWRENCE** comes from English/Irish stock. She was born and brought up in north Wales. She returned there when she married, and her sons were both born on Anglesey, an island off the coast. Though not isolated, Anglesey is a little off the beaten track, but lively Dublin, which Kim loves, is only a short ferry ride away.

Today, they live on the farm her husband was brought up on. Welsh is the first language of many people in this area, and Kim's husband and sons are all bilingual—she is having a lot of fun, not to mention a few headaches, trying to learn the language!

With small children, she thought the unsocial hours of nursing weren't attractive, so—encouraged by a husband who thinks she can do anything she sets her mind to—Kim tried her hand at writing. Always a keen reader of Harlequin books, it seemed natural for her to write a romance novel. Now she can't imagine doing anything else.

She is a keen gardener and cook and enjoys running—often on the beach, as on an island the sea is never very far away. She is usually accompanied by her Jack Russell, Sprout—don't ask, it's a long story!

A SPANISH AWAKENING
KIM LAWRENCE

~ One Night In... ~

TORONTO NEW YORK LONDON
AMSTERDAM PARIS SYDNEY HAMBURG
STOCKHOLM ATHENS TOKYO MILAN MADRID
PRAGUE WARSAW BUDAPEST AUCKLAND

Recycling programs
for this product may
not exist in your area.

ISBN-13: 978-0-373-52821-9

A SPANISH AWAKENING

First North American Publication 2011

Copyright © 2011 by Kim Lawrence

A SPANISH AWAKENING

CHAPTER ONE

EMILIO swallowed his coffee, grimacing at the taste. It had gone cold. Knotting his silk tie with one hand, he finished up the coffee and headed out of the door. A quick glance at his watch confirmed that with luck and good traffic he could make it to the airport to meet Rosanna's flight and still be at his desk by ten—a very late start for him, but being the boss did have certain privileges.

There were people who considered his life was one long privilege.

Some went further, like the actress he had been meant to escort to a premiere the previous night. She had called him selfish—quite loudly.

Emilio had received the insult with a philosophical smile. Her good opinion meant nothing to him. They had not even slept together yet and he doubted now they would, even though she had rung back later, clearly regretting her outburst, to apologise.

Her efforts to ingratiate herself had left him as unmoved as her earlier tantrum. He actually thought she might have a point—maybe he was selfish. The possibility did not unduly bother him. Was selfishness not the upside of being single and not in a serious relationship?

Upside? Were there any downsides to being in a position where one did not have to consider the wishes of other people? Emilio could not think of any.

In the past he had done his duty and pleased others, namely his father. That unquestioning compliance had resulted in a failed marriage entered into when he was too young, stupid and arrogant to believe he could fail at anything.

On paper his father had been right. He and Rosanna had been the perfect couple, they had a lot in common, they came from the same world, and, most importantly from his father's point of view, his bride had been good breeding stock from a family who could trace their bloodline back *almost* as far as his own family.

Emilio slid into the driving seat of his car, his lips twisting into a bitter smile of recollection as he fastened his seat belt.

Luis Rios had been incoherent with outrage when the marriage he had promoted had failed. He had used every threat and bullying tactic in his considerable arsenal and had become frustrated when he saw none made any impression on his son.

His fury had turned to scornful contempt when Emilio had introduced the topic of love, suggesting mildly that the absence of it might be a possible reason for the short life span of the doomed marriage.

The irony in his voice had sailed—predictably—directly over his father's head.

'Love?' his parent had snorted contemptuously. 'Is that what this is about? Since when were *you* a romantic?'

The question had, Emilio conceded, been legitimate. It was true that his own attitude towards the hype around romantic love had always been at best condescending, at worst contemptuous.

He had continued to feel that way right up to the moment

he had found out the hard way that love was not an invention of overactive imaginations, that it was possible to look at a woman and know with every fibre of your being that she was *meant* to be yours.

The instant was indelibly seared into Emilio's memory, every individual detail of her breathless late arrival midway through the boring dinner carrying the scent of the warm summer night into the stuffy room with her.

His heart had literally stopped, which was crazy when you considered how many times he had seen her walk into a room previously, but in that moment it had been as if he were seeing her for the first time.

Wary of sliding into self-pitying mode, jaw clenched, Emilio pushed away the image of her face allowing the far less pleasing image of his father's face to fill the space it left. He no longer attempted to fill the empty space in his heart; he lived with it.

You didn't lose her, he reminded himself. She was never yours. Because the fact was it was all about timing and his had stunk.

He crunched the gears, wincing at the sound as he heard his father say, 'If you want *love*, take a mistress. Take several.' His father had sounded astonished that such an obvious solution had not occurred to his son.

Emilio could still remember looking at the man who had fathered him and feeling not even filial duty—there had never been affection—but coruscating revulsion that burnt through his veins like acid.

The idea of putting anyone through the humiliation his father had inflicted on his mother had filled Emilio with deep repugnance. Emilio might have entered into a marriage of convenience, but he had always intended to be faithful.

'Like you did, Papa?' It had been a tremendous struggle

to keep his voice level, but he had not struggled to disguise the anger and disgust he felt.

The older man had been the first to look away, but during that long moment their eyes had met a profound change had taken place in the relationship between father and son.

Luis Rios had never attempted to carry through with any of his threats to disown him, but Emilio would not have cared if he had. Part of him would have relished the challenge of building a life away from the financial empire his great-grandfather had begun and each successive generation had built upon.

It had been shortly after this event that his father had stopped taking any active part in the business, retiring to the stud where he bred racehorses, leaving Emilio free to put in place wide-ranging changes with no opposition. Changes that meant the global financial downturn had left the Rios brand virtually untouched and the envy of many rivals. People had begun to speak enviously of the Rios luck.

That luck appeared to be working in his favour as he drove into what appeared to be the only vacant parking space a full ten minutes before his ex-wife's flight was due in.

Emilio walked towards the terminal building feeling glad as he passed by a group of vociferous placard-carrying air-traffic controllers that he was not here to catch a flight. The building was filled with anxious and, to varying degrees, angry people who clearly were.

He spared a sympathetic thought for them before his thoughts turned to the reason for his presence. He sighed, wishing he shared Philip's apparent belief that one word from him would somehow magically remove any obstacle in his friend's path to romantic fulfillment. Still, some of the things his friend had said had made it seem that there were things that had been left unsaid.

Emilio had not seen Philip Armstrong for almost a year, so it had been a surprise to see his old friend walk into his office yesterday.

Emilio gave a sardonic smile—it had not been the last!

He chose a vantage point where he would see Rosanna and allowed his thoughts to drift back over yesterday's extraordinary conversation.

'There is a problem.'

It was not a question. A person did not have to be an expert at reading body language to see that there was something wrong in Philip's world.

'I've never been happier.'

The gloomy reply made Emilio's lips twitch. 'It does not show.'

'I've fallen in love, Emilio.' If anything, the Englishman's gloom seemed even more pronounced as he explained the source of his great joy.

'Congratulations.'

Missing the sardonic inflection, Philip produced a dour 'Thanks.' Adding, 'Oh, I don't expect *you* to believe it. I've often wondered, you know…?'

'What have you wondered?' Emilio asked, mystified but not inclined to take umbrage from the underlying antagonism that had crept into the other man's manner.

'Why did you ever get married?' he said bitterly. 'It's not as if you were—'

'In love?' Emilio suggested without heat. 'No, I was not. I am presuming you did not come here to discuss my marriage.'

'Actually, I did, sort of,' Philip Armstrong conceded. 'The thing is, Emilio…'

Emilio repressed his impatience.

'The thing is, I want to get married,' the Englishman revealed in a rush.

'That is surely good news?'

'I want to marry your wife.'

Emilio was famed for his powers of analytical deduction, but he had not seen this one coming!

'You're shocked. I knew you would be,' his old school friend announced with darkly pessimistic gloom.

'I am surprised,' Emilio corrected honestly. 'But if I was shocked, would it matter? Rosanna has not been my wife for quite some time. You do not require my blessing or my permission.'

'I know, but the thing is I think she feels guilty about finding happiness.'

'I think you are imagining things,' Emilio said, wondering if he ought not at some level to feel a little jealous.

He didn't. He was still fond of Rosanna, but then that had been the problem: he had been *fond* of Rosanna just as she had been *fond* of him. It was one of the many things they had in common, and they had both agreed that mutual respect and common interests were a much stronger foundation for a successful marriage than anything as transitory as romantic love.

Madre di Dios, he really had been that stupid!

The marriage had, of course, been doomed, but Emilio had been spared the painful task of telling Rosanna that there was 'someone else'. He hadn't needed to agonise over it, she had taken one look at him and known.

Women's intuition, or had he been that obvious?

What he had not been spared was the overriding sense of guilt—irrational, some might have said, considering his wife had been already unfaithful to him—that and the nasty taste that came with failure in any form.

It had been drummed into Emilio in his cradle that an integral part of being a Rios was not contemplating failure. It was a lesson he had learnt well. Divorce was not just failure, it was public failure, and that had been tougher to take than his wife's confession she had slept with someone else months after they had exchanged vows.

Emilio had been a lot more tolerant of her weakness than he had his own, and in his eyes the fact he had not been physically unfaithful did not make him any less culpable.

Before issuing the public statement on the divorce they had told their respective families, to prepare them. His father's reaction had been predictable and Emilio had been able to view his final ranting condemnation with an air of detached distaste that had clearly incensed his parent further.

What had been far less predictable was the viciously hostile response of Rosanna's family—that had been a genuine shock to him, but not, quite clearly, to her.

It had come out during the heated exchange that unbeknown to him his father had agreed to pay the blue-blooded but broke Carreras family a large sum of money on the marriage and another equally large sum when the first offspring of that union was born.

Under the impression that her attitude had been similar to his own when they had married, he could now see that his bride's motivation had been less to do with pragmatism and more to do with coercion and parental pressure.

It certainly explained Rosanna's initial refusal of a divorce when he had floated it. At the time he had been mystified, but now he realised that she was more afraid of being disowned by her money-grabbing family than living a lie.

It was the reason that, though supporting the official line of mutual decision, amicable divorce, blah...blah, Emilio had not made any effort to deny the rumours that had hinted heavily that his infidelity had caused the rift.

It was not totally a lie and it made things easier on Rosanna, as did the sum he paid the Carreras family out of his own funds.

The media, having created the story, had waited, headlines at the ready, confidently anticipating a lover or lovers to surface once they realised their sordid stories were lucrative. Of course none had because the person he had left his wife for remained oblivious to her role in these events.

Any woman seen with him immediately after the divorce would run the risk of being labelled the other woman, but patience in the circumstances was, he had reasoned, if not a virtue, certainly a necessity if he wanted to protect the reputation of the woman he had fallen for.

So he had waited a decent interval, or almost—there were limits to his patience—before he made any move: six months for the divorce to be finalised and six months for the dust to settle. The only minor problem he'd anticipated that day had been his inexperience at courtship; Emilio knew about seduction but he had never wooed a woman.

The dark irony of it almost drew a laugh from him— almost. It was hard to smile at anything related to the day he had had his heart broken and his pride crushed simultaneously.

In hindsight he was now able to appreciate that the injury to his pride had caused the most damage. He was embarrassed that for a short time he had done the predictable bitter and railing-at-fate thing, but he had reined in those emotions, walled them securely up—a man had to put a time limit on such self-indulgences—and got on with his life.

There had been a certain dark irony in Philip's comment of, 'If you could fall in love with someone, I'm sure Rosanna could move on.'

'With anyone in particular?'

'God, no, anyone would do.' Emilio's laughter brought his attention back to his friend's face. 'Sorry,' he said with a self-conscious grimace. 'I've had a sense of humour bypass. It's just I know we could be happy, but Rosanna— I think she won't be able to move on until you're with someone…'

'I have hardly spent the last two years living the existence of a monk.'

'I know that and I'm sure most men would envy you,' Philip admitted. 'I did. The thing is, Rosanna thinks that underneath you're not really that shallow, not that I think you're shallow.'

'I'm relieved,' Emilio responded gravely. 'So you are asking me to fall in love to make your love life easier. I'm sorry, Philip. I would do a lot for you but—'

'I know. I don't know what I expected. The thing is I'm pretty desperate.' The driven expression shining in his blue eyes was a reflection of that desperation. 'I'd do anything for Rosanna—cut my hair, for starters.'

The comment drew a laugh from Emilio. 'I am impressed.'

'I'm serious. It's time to settle down. No more wandering the world for me. I'm going to get respectable. If Rosanna wants me to, I'd even go and work for Dad, become a suit, swallow the silver spoon and be the son he always wanted me to be.'

'Would the opportunity arise?'

'Are you kidding? Dad would love it if I came crawling back with my tail between my legs. He's built up his empire to hand it over to his heir.' He grinned and directed a finger at his own chest. 'Me.'

'You are hardly an only child.'

Philip conceded this point with a shrug. 'I suppose if Janie had been interested in the business the fatted calf might not await me, but she never was and it's not likely she will be, having become the face of that perfume. It's real spooky to see your little sister staring at you from magazine covers and advertising boards.'

Emilio dismissed the elder of the Armstrong sisters with a shake of his head. 'I was thinking of Megan.'

The sight of a familiar figure snapped him back to the present, catching his gaze as he scanned the busy concourse searching for his ex-wife.

He had thought of Megan and now she was here!

Despite the fact she appeared to have dropped a couple of dress sizes—a circumstance he did not totally approve of—and acquired a fashionable gloss to match the new poise in her manner, he knew Megan Armstrong immediately.

Of course he knew her. Emilio, not a man given to exaggeration, believed totally he could have located her blindfolded in a room of a thousand beautiful Englishwomen!

It was enough, he reflected, to make a man believe in fate. Of course, Emilio did not believe in signs or cosmic forces, but he did believe in following his instincts.

If he followed his at that moment it might get them both arrested. A smile that did not soften the predatory glow in his eyes flickered across his face as he thought, It might be worth it.

CHAPTER TWO

'BUT I need you here tonight!'

Megan was not surprised to hear the aggrieved note tinged with truculence in her boss's voice.

Charlie Armstrong had not made his millions by allowing little things like air-traffic controllers' strikes to stand in his way and he expected his staff to display an equally robust response to such obstacles to his wishes, even when that member of staff was his daughter.

Actually, *especially* when that employee was his daughter!

'Sorry, Dad.'

'What use is sorry to me? I need—'

'But it looks like I'm stuck here,' Megan inserted, her calm, unruffled tone affording a stark contrast to her father's haranguing bellow. 'I'll book into a hotel here and catch the first flight out tomorrow,' she promised.

'And when will that be?'

Megan glanced at the slightly scratched face of the watch that encircled her slim wrist. Not an expensive item but as far as Megan was concerned utterly invaluable, it had belonged to her mother, who had died when she was twelve.

'It's a twenty-four-hour strike so 9:00 a.m. tomorrow is the earliest flight.'

'Nine! No, that is simply not acceptable!'

'Acceptable or not, Dad, short of sprouting wings I'm grounded, and before you suggest it, the trains and cross-channel ferries are booked up.'

'By people with foresight.'

Megan resisted the impulse to retort by people who were returning home after the international football tournament, knowing that an excuse, legitimate or not, would not soothe her father when he was in this mood.

She let him vent his displeasure loudly for another few minutes, responding with the occasional monosyllabic murmur of agreement when appropriate while she allowed herself to be carried along by the seething mass of bodies, fellow stranded travellers who were all heading in the same direction, towards the exit.

Getting a taxi was going to be a nightmare. Megan mentally prepared herself for a long wait. Maybe she should simply camp out in the airport overnight?

'And don't expect me to fork out for fancy hotels. Being my daughter doesn't mean you can take advantage of the situation. I expect the same level of commitment from you that I would expect from any of my—'

As she tuned out the lecture she had heard many times before Megan's attention strayed around the crowded space heaving with a cross-section of humanity.

The air left her lungs in a fractured gasp as recognition jolted through her body with the fizz of an electric shock. *'Oh, my God!'* she breathed, pressing a hand to her heaving chest.

'What? What is it?'

Megan squeezed her eyes shut, but still saw the face that had caused her to haemorrhage the composure that had become her trademark.

It was not a face that was easy to banish!

She took a deep breath, looking up in guilty acknowledgement towards the young man who had nearly tripped over her when she had come to a dead halt without warning. 'I'm so sorry.'

'No problems,' said the backpacker, losing his air of irritation and producing an engaging smile as he took in her slim figure, gleaming, glossy brown hair and English-rose heart-shaped face. 'Do you want a hand with that bag?'

Megan, who was already drifting away, didn't register the offer as she glanced back towards the door through which she had seen the tall figure framed, her emotions a mixture of heart-thudding excitement and trepidation.

It was empty.

Had she imagined it? Her glance swung to left and right, moving over the swathe of heads. Emilio Rios was not the sort of man who blended into a crowd.

'What is it, Megan? What's wrong?'

'Nothing, Dad, I'm fine,' she lied, well aware that her reaction to someone who bore a fleeting similarity to someone who probably had forgotten she existed had been, to put it mildly, way over the top.

'Well, you don't sound fine!'

It was mortifying. In a matter of seconds she had regressed to the cringingly naïve and self-conscious twenty-one-year-old she had been the last time she had seen him. If her feet had not been nailed to the floor she would have turned and run, exactly the way she had eventually done on that occasion.

Now how crazy was that?

She had not seen the man for almost two years and he had probably forgotten both her and the rather embarrassing circumstances of their last meeting.

All the same, she was glad she had only imagined him.

Megan took evasive action to avoid a baggage trolley

being wheeled straight at her before replying to her father's comment. 'It was nothing. I just thought I saw someone, that's all. Look, I'll have to go now. I'll ring you later when I've booked in somewhere.'

'Saw who?'

Megan took a deep breath and swallowed, the name emerging huskily from her dry throat. 'Emilio Rios.'

'Emilio!'

'Or someone who looked like him.' This was Madrid. There were a lot of dark, dramatically handsome men; some were even several inches over six feet. Why assume that man she had seen for a split second had been him? It could have been anyone.

The realisation made some of the tension leave her shoulders.

'No, it could be him, you know,' her father mused. 'He has an office in Madrid.'

It would have been harder to mention a capital where there was not a building bearing the Rios name. Emilio was accounted by some in the financial world to be a genius, by others to be incredibly lucky.

In Megan's opinion, to be as successful as he was he had to be both, with the added essential ingredient of utter ruthlessness thrown in!

The tension back with bells on, Megan heard her father add, 'The Rios family estate is nearby, magnificent old place.' The awe in the voice of a man who lived in a stately pile with more rooms than Megan had ever counted suggested the Rios Estate really was something out of the ordinary.

'Well, if he was here he's gone now,' she said as much for her own benefit as her dad's.

'I stayed there once when Luis and I were negotiating

a deal. My God, that man was slippery. Did you ever meet Emilio's father?'

'I thought he was a bit of a snob, actually.'

'No, not a snob,' her father disagreed, sounding irritated by her outspoken appraisal. 'Just very old-school and immensely proud of his family heritage, and who can blame him? They can trace their history back centuries. You know, this Madrid stopover of yours might not be such a bad thing after all.'

Deeply distrustful of the thoughtful note in her father's voice, Megan frowned and said warily, 'You think so?'

'I'll ring Emilio.'

A loud announcement on the speaker system drowned out Megan's wailed protest of, 'Oh, God, no, don't do that!'

'I've lost touch since Luis retired. This could be the perfect opportunity to reconnect, and I'm sure Emilio could arrange accommodation for you.'

'I wouldn't want to trade on our relationship.'

Ignoring the sarcasm of her retort, Charles mused thoughtfully, 'The Rios family have strong South American connections, connections that could be very useful if the Ortega deal proves viable. Actually, even if it doesn't there are—'

Shaking her head, Megan cut her father off mid-flow. *'No.'*

'What do you mean?'

'I mean, no, I will not butter up Emilio Rios for you.'

'Did I ask you to?' her father said, sounding suitably bewildered and hurt by the accusation.

'Emilio Rios was Philip's friend, not mine. *I* don't even like the man.' Two years ago he had been well on the way to becoming a carbon copy of his aristocratic, aloof father. By now he had probably become equally stuffy and pretentious.

There was nothing like being lauded as a genius to confirm a person's belief in his own infallibility, and having beautiful women throw themselves at your feet was not exactly going to encourage humility, she reflected sourly.

'You used to follow him around like a puppy.'

The reminder brought a flush to her cheeks. 'I'm not twelve, Dad.' Actually, she had been thirteen when her brother had brought home his college friend, who had been the most beautiful young man she had ever imagined, let alone laid eyes on.

He had been kind.

Later he had been cruel.

'And anyway, he *definitely* doesn't like me.' This was not a stab in the dark; it was actually an understatement. Two years on the memory of his blighting scorn no longer had the power to make her feel physically sick. Though she was a little way off laughing at it.

'Don't be stupid, Megan. Why would he not like you? I doubt if you even registered on his radar back then.'

Is that meant to make me feel better? Megan wondered.

'I did have hopes he might have fallen for Janie.'

Why not? Megan thought. Everyone else had, or so it had seemed to her when she had watched, with wistful envy, her beautiful half-sister make male jaws drop wherever she went.

'But I think that marriage of his was a done deal when they were both in their cradles. But that's over and it's different now. You've turned into quite an attractive young woman. No Janie, obviously.'

Obviously, Megan thought, and her twisted smile was more philosophical than cynical as she said, 'You mean I lost twenty pounds.' There was less of her but suddenly she was a lot more visible, at least to male eyes. 'Look, Dad, I have to— Hold on, Dad,' she added, turning in response to the pressure of a hand on her shoulder.

The expression of polite enquiry on her face melted into one of wild-eyed panic as she tilted her face up at the man standing at her shoulder.

He was the reason why she was suddenly not being jostled. People did not jostle Emilio Rios. It wasn't just his physical presence, which was considerable, it was his aura.

'You!' Oh, God, how long had he been standing there? The thought that he had been listening made her feel queasy.

Emilio Rios smiled and Megan's lips parted. She had no control over the tiny sigh of female appreciation that emerged from her throat. Fortunately the level of noise in the place drowned it out.

The smile did not reach his dark eyes, just deepened the fine lines fanning out from the corners, leaving the gleaming depths intent as without a word he framed her face with his big hands.

A myriad emotions swirling in jumbled psychedelic chaos through her head, Megan stood immobile as she felt the warm brush of his breath against the fluttering pulse at the base of her neck, then the downy softness of her cheek as his dark features blurred out of focus as she struggled to escape the magnetic tug of his unblinking stare.

Logic told her this was not happening, but it was. This wasn't a dream; it was real. Dreams were not hot; he was. Across the inches barely separating them the heat of his body seeped through the fine creased linen of her jacket.

Say something! Do something?

She did neither, but he did.

Emilio bent his head and covered her mouth with his.

Scream, kick him, bite him, said the voice in her head.

Instead she melted into him, her soft body moulding sinuously against the lean, hard length of him. Her lips parted with a silent sigh, not just allowing but inviting the bold, erotic penetration of his tongue.

Need and enervating lust rolled over her, sweeping her along in its wake as she clung to him, her arms sliding around his middle.

The crowds faded, her sense of self faded, all that remained was the taste of him filling her mouth, the texture of his warm lips. The hunger inside her responding with mindless enthusiasm to the erotic probing advances of his tongue.

Then just as abruptly as it had begun it stopped and she was standing there deprived of the heat of his body, shaking and feeling pretty much as if she had just been run over by a truck.

Megan's hands balled into fists at her sides.

'Mr Rios,' she croaked. 'I was just talking about you.' She raised the phone that she still held in a white-knuckled grip.

He just kissed you!

Two years had not changed him. He looked perhaps a little leaner, a little harder, the angles and planes of his incredible face perhaps more sharply defined, but essentially he was still the same.

But you're not that Megan, you've moved on, she reminded herself.

He just kissed you.

Emilio stood waiting for his breathing to return to something approximating normal and watched her, fascinated to see denial this close up. Megan was addressing her remarks to some point over his left shoulder and her attractive contralto voice had an audible edge of hysteria. The open neck of her blouse didn't quite hide the pulse that beat at the base of her throat.

Struggling to control the hunger rampaging through his body, he avoided looking at her mouth, deciding it would not help the painful issue of his arousal, which remained painfully obvious—also painful!

Kissing in public places had some definite disadvantages.

You've met a lot of good-looking men, Megan, she told herself. You can look at him and not turn into a gibbering idiot. You do not worship this man from afar. He cannot injure you with an unfair accusation and harsh word. He has no power at all over you any more because he's just a good-looking man you used to slightly know because he went to school with your brother.

Just a man who made it a struggle to breathe when she looked at him and all that scalp-tingling stuff. Her glance swept downwards as she rubbed her forearms to dispel the goose bumps that in the heat of the terminal building had broken out over her body like a rash.

Face it, Megan, a man like Emilio is never going to be just a man, not with a mouth like that. But that didn't mean she had to humiliate herself by drooling.

'I know, I heard you.'

Somewhere above the hum of noise and the pounding of her heart as it struggled to batter its way through her ribcage, Megan was conscious of a voice, a vaguely familiar voice, calling Emilio's name.

If he heard it he gave no sign, he just continued to stare silently down at her with an expression on his face that she struggled to interpret.

'You just kissed me.'

He angled a dark brow. 'I was beginning to think you hadn't noticed.'

'I'm ignoring it.' Or not dealing with it? 'Like I ignore troublesome, irritating bugs.'

'So you do not like me?'

The possibility did not appear to have dented his armour-plated confidence, she thought, struggling to recover her shredded composure, or at least close her mouth—it was so *not* a good look.

Relax, she told herself.

It was not *like* or anything similarly tepid that Emilio felt as his eyes moved across the soft contours of her upturned features. Soft was the right word, he decided, allowing his eyes to briefly drop as far as her visibly heaving bosom before returning to her face, soft and feminine.

The colour of her eyes had always fascinated him, a deep shade of topaz, though at this moment only a rim of that remarkable colour remained around her dilated pupils. Her skin was incredible. Under the spreading dark stain on her smooth cheeks it was milk-pale and totally flawless. Did that milky pallor extend all over?

He watched the muscles in her pale throat contract as she blinked and gave her glossy head a tiny shake and lifted her chin to a defiant angle before opening her eyes. Emilio, identifying the 'don't mess with me' look on her face, felt a buzz in his blood that had been absent for a long time as he silently accepted the challenge.

He would dearly love to mess with her.

Megan was familiar with powerful men and their generally fragile egos. Experience had taught her that great men's egos responded well to a well-chosen word. She had averted many a potential meltdown with a placatory word, a compliment.

This was a situation she was more than capable of coping with, which begged the question—why wasn't she? Why was she standing there like an idiot?

Powerful, successful men liked to be told they were wonderful as well as the next person—possibly more, because they took it as their due.

She took a deep breath that eased the tightness in her aching chest, opened her mouth and heard herself say, 'No. No, I don't like you at all.' Not the sop to his ego she had intended.

'You do not know me, although you think you do.'

Megan's edginess materialised as hostility as she tilted her chin. 'Very profound, but actually I don't want to know you,' she blurted childishly. 'And if you kiss me again I will—'

Emilio arched a questioning brow and smiled down into her upturned face. 'You will what?' he enquired with interest.

Megan inhaled and thought, Good question. 'Just don't!'

Not a threat likely to make him gibber in fear, but it was preferable to the more candid response of, *Kiss you back!*

She watched his eyes glitter in response to the warning, not with anger, not with amusement, but with something else she could not put a name to. Megan struggled to keep her eyes on his face as the nameless something made her stomach dissolve into a liquid, molten mush.

'That came from the heart.'

Aware that the organ in question was trying to batter its way through her ribs, she glared at him.

Megan heard his name again and began to turn her head towards the sound, but a long brown finger laid against the curve of her jaw prevented her.

The unexpected contact sent a shudder through her body and dragged a shocked breath from her lungs.

She wanted to slap his hand away.

She wanted to tell him she had no desire to know him.

She wanted to tell him to stop looking at her like that.

'Stop looking—'

As his mouth covered her own for a second time the strength left Megan's body in one whoosh. If one hand had not curled like a supportive steel band around her ribcage, dragging her body up against his iron-hard thighs, she would have slid to the ground.

When he released her she was breathing hard as she blinked up at him. 'I told you not to do that.'

'What can I say? It's the challenge and also your mouth. It was made for kissing.'

Taking the phone from her grasp, Emilio lifted it to his ear and, still holding her eyes, spoke into the mouthpiece.

'Rios here.'

Megan slanted an angry glare at his face and held out her hand.

'Ah, Charles. Yes, she is here with me now,' Emilio said, ignoring her silent demand, and continued to speak, responding to what her father was saying, his voice oozing almost as much insincerity as his mocking gaze.

'No, don't worry, I will take care of her. No need, it is not a problem, Charles.' A taunting grin in place on his lean face, Emilio turned to evade the hand that tried to snatch the phone from him. He waved an admonishing finger at her face and directed a wolfish smile at her indignant face as he raised his voice and said, 'It is a total pleasure and no trouble at all. Yes, and Megan sends her love.'

Love was not the emotion stamped on Megan's face

when she attracted the attention of several people within earshot as she yelled, 'No, I don't!'

Finally able to grab the phone, Megan snatched it from his hand and lifted it to her own ear, struggling to regain some semblance of control. 'Dad?' she said. 'I don't need to bother Mr Rios, I'm—I'm… He's gone,' she said, directing an accusing look up at Emilio's dark face.

'Your father is a busy man.'

'My father is—' Megan bit back the unflattering reading of her father's character and glared up at Emilio.

'He can relax now he knows you have someone to look after you.'

'I don't need anyone to look after me, and my father knows it. He just wants me to be nice to you because you have contacts that he…' Realising belatedly the extreme indiscretion of her goaded retort, she closed her lips firmly over further tactless disclosures.

Emilio's lips thinned as his nostrils flared in distaste. Who needed an enemy when you had a father like Charles Armstrong? A man who had never really grasped the fact that a father's duty to his children was to protect and shield.

Armstrong used anyone, including members of his own family, if it gave him an advantage.

'Just how nice does he expect you to be to me?'

Megan responded to the comment as if it had been a slap, catching her breath and drawing back. The subsequent blast of fury that sizzled along her nerve endings blinded Megan to the sympathy in Emilio's dark eyes.

She lifted her chin and glared up at him. 'My father does not ask me to have sex with men who can be useful to him.'

'Though he'd not be likely to kick up a fuss if you decided to.'

'I have sex with men because I want to.'

So far she had not wanted to, but Megan saw no reason to share this information with Emilio Rios; even if she had, she doubted he would have believed her.

Ironic, really—the world thought she was a bit of an iceberg, a reputation she found it comfortable to hide behind, but Emilio Rios thought she was some sort of sex-mad tart.

Two years ago her initial gratitude at being rescued from a situation that had escalated dangerously out of control had changed to wretched misery when he had looked at her with contempt and treated her to a blighting lecture on the dangers of leading men on.

Acting as though she were some sort of sexual predator!

Sexual predator!

At that point Megan hadn't even had a real boyfriend. The man Emilio had rescued her from had not been her date. He was a lecturer, quite old to her mind, and she had treated his kind offer of a lift home from the graduation party, when the boy who had promised her an early lift home had become drunk and incapable, as just that—kind.

How was she meant to have known that he had been drinking too? She hadn't had a clue until he had put his foot down through the village, then, after making her extremely uncomfortable with comments loaded with sexual innuendo, instead of taking her to the house where her father was hosting a party for his business partner—all the family were under orders to attend—he'd pulled up on the long tree-lined drive leading up to the house and tried to kiss her.

During the rather undignified tussle that had followed Megan had tried to remain calm, but she had been close to panic when the door had been dragged open to reveal Emilio.

Her relief had been short-lived.

'So how about me?'

She looked at him blankly as she pushed away the memory of that night. 'How about you what?'

Emilio arched a sardonic brow. 'Do you want to have sex with me?'

Heat flashed through Megan. She was insulted, she told herself, not excited. She hung on to her temper with difficulty and pretended to consider his insolent question. 'You got a spare million?' Word was he had several.

His brows lifted. 'You value yourself highly.'

Megan flicked the ponytail that lay against her neck and responded with a cool assurance she was about a million miles from feeling. 'I'm worth it.'

'Then maybe we could work something out. I'm not averse to paying for quality,' he drawled.

The sexual tension soared as they stared at one another, neither willing to back down. But before this absurd negotiation went any further a voice cut across the seething silence.

'Emilio?'

CHAPTER THREE

MEGAN turned her head. The woman standing there was tiny, barely an inch above five feet. The last time she had seen the petite brunette the older woman had been wearing a ring; today her hand was bare, but nothing else, it seemed, had changed.

Rosanna Rios was still the most beautiful woman she had ever met. Never a hair out of place, she looked like a porcelain ornament with big brown eyes, a rosebud mouth and delicate nose. She had the sort of delicate fragility that aroused the protective instincts in men.

'I did call, but you were...' she raised a darkened brow and lifted her enquiring gaze to Emilio as she teased '...occupied.'

Megan felt her stomach muscles tighten as she watched Emilio brush the smooth cheek offered him with his lips.

'I had no idea at all.' Rosanna turned to smile at Megan, adding with a smile tinged with relief as she turned back to Emilio, 'I'm glad things are finally working out for you.'

Megan, puzzling over the soft-voiced aside, waited for Emilio to set the record straight. Instead she heard him ask his ex-wife if she was being met.

'I was.' Rosanna scanned the crowds, a delicate frown

furrowing her smooth brow. 'But he appears to have been held up.'

'Can we offer you a lift?'

Megan, frowning at the *we* and the misleading message it sent, watched as Rosanna shook her head. 'I'll wait.'

Emilio shrugged and placed a hand lightly between Megan's shoulder blades, acting as if he hadn't noticed when she flinched. 'If you're sure?'

Megan flashed him a 'what the hell are you up to?' look, which he responded to by dropping his head to whisper softly in her ear, 'I'll meet your price.'

The mortified colour flew to Megan's cheeks as she blurted loudly, 'I wasn't serious and you know it.'

'You really shouldn't make offers you don't intend to follow through with,' he chided, adding, 'Sorry, Rosanna, we're being rude.'

'*You're* being rude,' Megan gritted.

Rude, and extremely manipulative.

'No apologies necessary. Are you two arriving? Or were you planning a romantic trip?'

'We are not together,' Megan protested in a belated attempt to set the record straight. The breathlessness of her delivery, due in part to the fingers that had begun to massage the tight area at the back of her neck, did not add weight to her claim.

The casual intimacy of his action sent a quiver of raw sexual awareness through her body.

Emilio hooked a thumb under her chin. 'You're tense, *querida*.' He disapproved with a frown that left his dark eyes warm with concern.

'I can't imagine why,' she retorted.

The ironic retort drew a laugh from Emilio, who allowed the hand that lay against her waist to slide lower to the firm curve of her bottom. 'Megan was planning to fly home, but it looks like I have her here for a little longer.'

Rosanna gave a sympathetic grimace. 'Bad luck.'

'Good luck for me.'

'I was lucky. I arrived on an early flight.'

'How long have you two been…?'

Megan, aware of Emilio's eyes on her face, struggled to manufacture an amused smile for the other woman. 'No, we're not, that is… He's joking.'

Emilio came to her rescue. 'We are just good friends,' he said with an 'if you believe that you'll believe anything' smile.

Rosanna smiled. 'Of course.'

'No, really we're…'

Emilio placed a finger to her lips.

The contact made her pupils dilate.

'Relax, Megan.' His deep voice, huskily suggestive of unspoken intimacies, shivered across her oversensitive nerve endings. 'Rosanna understands, and she is not going to report back to anyone,' he soothed, lifting a stray hank of hair from her cheek.

A hazy, distracted expression drifted across his face as he rubbed the silky strands between his fingers before tucking them behind her ear.

Megan swallowed and struggled to maintain a façade of calm while her thudding heart tried to climb its way out of her chest cavity.

Mesmerised, she stared at him. She did not register the time lapse before he pushed her hair from her face. She was too busy registering unpleasant things like the almost painful clutching of her stomach muscles and the rush of heat that raised her core temperature by several uncomfortable degrees.

His hand did not fall away. Instead he touched her ear

lobe, seeming to notice the amber studs in the gold setting for the first time. His dark, thickly lashed eyes drifted downwards to the hollow of her throat where a pulse fluttered visibly against the tender blue-veined white skin.

Any residual guilt he might have felt for exploiting the situation had long vanished. It had been a long time coming, but Megan Armstrong was going to be his and he was going to make her forget every man she had ever been with—and, *Madre di Dios*, he was going to enjoy every second of it!

His fingertips barely brushed her, but even the suggestion of contact sent a shiver of sensation across the surface of her skin. She was frozen to the spot by a wave of enervating lust that was terrifying in its strength.

Hating the feeling of being utterly helpless and not in control, Megan hid behind the sweeping half-moon fan of her dark lashes and, like a drowning man clinging to a straw, repeated, *You'll laugh about this later*, over and over in her head.

'I like those,' he said, making her shiver as he touched, not just the earring, but the thin layer of skin behind her ear, and Megan realised it really was an erogenous zone.

God, I've got erogenous zones!

She met his dark intent gaze and thought, God, I've got a problem!

Her hand came up to push his away—that had been the intention at least. Instead she somehow ended up with her fingers curled over his and stayed there for an awkward heart-thudding moment.

'They were my mum's.'

Her eyes dropped from his uncomfortably perceptive gaze a moment before they filled with emotional tears. The earrings were one of a handful of physical reminders she had of her mother, along with her watch and the creased and grainy snapshot of herself as a baby held in her mother's arms she carried in her wallet.

'They match your eyes. Did your mother have golden eyes too?' His voice flowed over her like honey.

She was startled by the question; the eyes in question flew to his. He wasn't really interested, she told herself. This little byplay was presumably for Rosanna's benefit— like the kisses.

'Yes, she did. I…I look like her.'

'Then she must have been a very beautiful woman.'

Megan felt her heart give a traitorous thud and forced herself to look away. He looked genuine but he was about as sincere as a politician running for re-election; she would be a fool if she lost sight of that fact.

Twisting her earring, she turned to the older woman. 'Look, it was nice to see you again but I'm running late.'

'Of course, and it was very nice to see you too, Megan,' she said warmly. 'Philip often speaks of you.'

'You speak to Philip?'

A look of consternation crossed the older woman's face. 'I, well—'

Emilio cut across her. 'I hate to interrupt, ladies, but—' he tapped the face of the watch on his wrist and angled a significant look at Megan '—this is why we are running late. You talk too much.' Grabbing her arm, he dropped a kiss on Rosanna's cheek and headed for the exit, virtually dragging Megan along with him.

She angled an angry look up at his lean face. 'What do you think you're doing?'

'I am rescuing you from an awkward situation.'

Megan loosed an incredulous hoot as they emerged in the fresh air. She pulled away from him and stood, hands on hips, glaring at him.

'An awkward situation of your making.'

He flashed a grin and held out an arm towards her. 'The car is this way.'

Megan didn't move. 'Goodbye.'

He studied her face for a moment before sighing. 'Look, we can—'

'Do this the hard way or the easy way,' she slotted in.

'Tempting, but no, I was going to say we can stand here debating this, but in the end you will accept a lift because the alternative is a very long wait.' He nodded towards the long queues beside the empty taxi ranks. 'And you are, I am led to believe, a practical woman not given to cutting off her very pretty nose to spite her beautiful face.

'Besides, I promised your father I would take care of you.'

'And you are a man of your word?'

'It hurts me you doubt it.' The silence stretched as he watched her struggle. 'Of course, if for some reason you are afraid to get in a car with me…?'

Her chin went up. 'Of course I'm not afraid,' she scoffed.

CHAPTER FOUR

ANGRY that she had allowed herself to be manipulated into accepting this lift—a two-year-old could have seen through his tactics—Megan maintained her tight-lipped, frigid silence until Emilio had negotiated the congested traffic around the airport.

'I think you owe me an apology.'

'You do? For what exactly?' he said, sounding interested.

'You kissed me.' Annoyingly, she could not say it without blushing. She just hoped he was too busy avoiding some suicidal cyclists to notice.

Emilio arched a brow and flashed a quick wolfish grin in her direction. 'I have not forgotten. You expect me to apologise for kissing you?'

Megan shook her head. 'I've already forgotten the actual kiss,' she lied, hoping but not expecting to bruise his ego. 'I expect you to apologise for using me that way to make your ex jealous.'

Emilio looked startled by the interpretation. 'Jealous?'

'And all that effort and it didn't even work. Face it, Emilio, she didn't care.' Possibly, Megan mused bitterly, because Rosanna knew all she had to do was click her pretty fingers and Emilio would come running. 'I have to admit I'm disappointed.'

'With my kissing?'

Megan, who had no intention of going there, ignored the interruption. 'I thought you were supposed to be the great authority on women, a regular Casanova…'

'You seem to take a great interest in my sex life.'

The taunt brought a flush of colour to her cheeks, but Megan didn't drop her gaze as she countered, 'It's hard to avoid it.'

He looked momentarily confused before his mouth twisted into a grimace. 'That damned article. How long is that damned thing going to haunt me?'

The look of disgust that flashed across his face made her laugh.

'Haunt?' she said, pretending confusion. 'I thought it was very flattering. Some of the things she said you did I didn't know were physically possible. May I give you some advice?'

'If that advice is don't sleep with women who confide intimate details to tabloids and trashy magazines, don't waste your breath.'

Emilio took very little interest in what was written about him, good or bad, but he was actually a long way from feeling the amused indifference his manner suggested, for this particular article had been, not only incredibly tasteless and salacious, but totally untrue.

He would have won any prosecution he brought against the magazine that published it, but such a course would have inevitably prolonged the public interest. Instead he had bitten the bullet and chosen to remain silent on the subject, waiting for it to go away.

'It wasn't,' Megan admitted. 'But it seems sound advice.'

'Only if you actually did sleep with the woman in question.'

Something in Emilio's voice brought her frowning scrutiny to his face. 'And you didn't,' she realised. 'But she said…?'

'And you believe everything you read in trashy magazines?' he asked sardonically.

'No…' she conceded doubtfully.

'Just everything you read about me?'

Megan aimed a killer look at his profile. The man, she brooded darkly, always had to have the last word.

'That advice—what was it? I would like to hear it, if only to prove to you that I actually have an open mind. So what pearl of wisdom would you like to share with me?'

'You want to know? Fine! I'm no expert—'

Emilio gave a lazy smile. 'I can feel a *but* coming on.'

'Do you want to hear what I have to say or not?'

He produced an unrealistically meek expression and mimed a zipping motion across his lips.

'*But*—it seems to me that kissing someone else is not the best way to win back a wife.'

There was a long silence before he filled it.

'You really think that is why I kissed you?' The next time he intended to make his intentions clearer—always easier when you didn't have several hundred people watching you.

She arched a brow and adopted an expression of amusement. Inside the laughter was noticeably absent as she said, 'And you're trying to tell me you were just overcome with uncontrollable lust when you saw me?'

Not for the first time she wondered what it would be like to be one of those women who did just that to men. Did that make her very shallow?

'I suppose you know that it was totally pathetic. I should

have called Security!' Instead I kissed you back, which was a really great idea.

'People kiss in airports.'

'Not like that!'

'You did not exactly beat me off with a stick.' Emilio struggled to concentrate on the road ahead as the memory of her soft curves moulding themselves to his body rose up to torment him.

'Quite the opposite. Now, why was that, I wonder?'

'I felt sorry for you.' Pleased with the way the explanation had tripped off her tongue, she added, 'You know, you really should get a life for real. Rosanna clearly has.'

Actually it wasn't at all clear. Megan could see that Emilio would be a hard act for any man to follow, even the most self-confident of men.

'Yes, she has. I believe we will be getting an invite to her wedding any day now.'

'She's getting married!' This information went a long way to explain Emilio's performance, especially if he was still in love with his ex-wife.

Megan squashed the flash of sympathy she felt for him. It might explain why, but it did not begin to excuse the way he had used her.

'It is in the cards, though not certain as yet. You sound surprised?'

'I am.'

Not as surprised as she had been when she had learnt that the couple who had seemed a perfect match on every level were breaking up. Up until the moment that the divorce had been announced Megan had anticipated a dramatic reconciliation, but the Rios divorce, like the break-up, had been low-key and bizarrely amicable based on what they called a mutual decision.

But had that mutual, civilized, still-good-friends routine

been a way to save face? The Rios family name came not only with a clearly superb gene pool, she thought, sweeping a covert glance through her lashes at Emilio's clear-cut patrician profile, but also some far less attractive things.

Things like family tradition and pride. How would divorce have gone down? In many ways the Rios family had not moved on very far from the Dark Ages, and they didn't do divorce. When it came to pride the Rios family had a lot more than their fair share.

For the first time she found herself wondering just how mutual the divorce had really been. Had it in reality been forced on him?

She flashed a speculative look at Emilio's profile, wondering if he too had been anticipating a passionate reconciliation?

'I thought marriage to you would have put her off the institution for life! It's almost as much of a mystery as why she married you in the first place.'

'Is it?' he said, looking at her mouth.

The insolent scrutiny made Megan shift uneasily in her seat. 'She seems quite sane.'

He continued to stare at her mouth until, unable to bear it a second longer, Megan yelled, 'Will you keep your eyes on the road?' They were stopped at a set of lights. 'And nobody gets married to someone because they are a good kisser, if that's what you're implying.'

'I am relieved you noticed. Actually, my talents extend beyond kissing.'

Megan dragged a hand jerkily down the front of her blouse, growing more agitated by the second. 'I really don't want to know!' she choked, dropping the pretence of an amused façade.

Her directive stemmed the flow of details, but not the

flow of visual examples of his *talent* slipping through her head.

'I should have waited for a taxi,' she muttered under her breath. 'God alone knows why I got in a car with you.'

'Possibly because you were hoping I'd kiss you again?'

Her slender shoulder lifted in a shrug and she sneered, 'No audience here, so I feel safe.'

He lifted one shoulder, but admitted modestly, 'I am not the exhibitionist you appear to think. I actually do some of my best work in private.'

His deep, throaty drawl sent Megan's imagination into free fall. She gasped as shameful heat flooded the sensitive juncture between her legs. 'Not with me!' she retorted as she pressed a button to open the window, pressing it again with a certain amount of desperation when it did not immediately respond.

'We do have air conditioning, you know.'

Megan stuck her head out of the window and breathed deeply. 'It's not working.' She found it extremely doubtful that a cold shower would have worked for her at that moment.

She was bewildered and alarmed by the ease with which he could arouse her physically. It was bizarre, but the excitement in her veins seemed to grow in direct proportion to the antagonism she felt towards him.

Emilio shifted gears and the powerful monster he drove shot forward, straining at the leash as the traffic began to move once more. He felt some sympathy for the machine's frustration; his libido was straining at the leash.

'You know what they say, *querida*—never say never.' His sideways glance touched her heaving bosom. 'You gave every appearance of enjoying yourself when you kissed me.' Her response had delighted him.

'That was not a kiss.'

'It was not?'

Megan chewed fretfully at her full lower lip and stared stubbornly out of the window. 'It was…a reflex,' she retorted in a driven voice.

'Indeed. I can only say that you have the best…*reflexes* of any woman I have ever come across.'

The window beckoned again.

When she pulled her head back in she pushed the mesh of hair from her eyes and observed with a spite that was totally uncharacteristic for her, 'I should have told Rosanna that, far from being an *item*—like anyone is going to believe that,' she inserted with a scornful sniff. 'I can't stand the sight of you!'

'Is it such a good idea to allow this to become personal?'

Megan stared at his patrician profile in disbelief. Was the man for real? 'It already is personal. It got personal the moment you k…k…you kissed me!'

'I too have excellent reflexes.'

Lips compressed, she directed her gaze on her hands clenched primly in her lap, thinking, Do not go there, Megan. 'I just bet you do,' she snarled, watching her knuckles blench white.

She flashed him a look of exasperation. 'Is it so impossible for you to believe that I can't stand the sight of you?'

'I believe that your reaction to me is not mild, and neither, for the record, is mine to you.' Before she could analyse the message within his cryptic utterance he continued, 'But I was referring to your comment…something along the lines of—"like anyone would believe that." Why would anyone *not* believe that we are lovers?'

Megan slung him an irritated look. 'I have a brain and

I like to be exclusive. Also I look nothing like a Barbie doll.'

'Ouch! So much for sisterly solidarity! You really should not judge by appearances, Megan.'

'You're right, *I'm* the superficial one.'

His grin flashed and her own smile faded. It would be an exaggeration to call the spiky atmosphere warm, but she was conscious that a worrying element of intimacy had developed.

Megan could have done without knowing he could laugh at himself; it made despising him all the more of a struggle. She needed out of this car and fast! God only knew what had possessed her to get in to begin with.

Like you don't know?

Ignoring the unhelpful contribution of the knowing voice in her head, she cut short the inner dialogue and said, 'Look, you can drop me at the first hotel we pass, if that's not a problem?' If it was a problem she could always jump out of the moving vehicle. It could not be a more painful experience than this conversation.

'Without feeding you first?' He shook his dark head in reproach.

'That really isn't necessary. I ate breakfast,' she lied brightly. 'And it isn't lunchtime.' She glanced at her watch and realised it was barely nine-thirty. It felt as though she had been in the car for hours.

His dark brows twitched into a straight line above his hawkish nose. 'You are very hung up with time,' he drawled.

'And you must be a very unique billionaire businessman if you have time to snack and watch the grass grow,' she retorted tartly.

'I work, but I am not a slave to routine.'

'Congratulations on being a free spirit, but I'm still not hungry.'

'You think your time would be put to better use counting the minutes until the planes start flying again? You're stuck here—I suggest you make the most of it. Madrid is a beautiful city, though being a native I must admit to some prejudice on the subject,' he conceded with a fluid shrug. 'Do you like architecture, history…?'

'Why—are you offering to be my guide?' She leaned back in her seat and thought, Gotcha, as she wondered how long it would take him to discover a very full diary.

It might amuse Emilio Rios to buy her breakfast, he might even feel he was obliged to do so because of her manipulative parent's request to look after her, but spending an entire day with her would definitely not be his idea of an efficient use of his time.

'Why not?'

The cynical smile playing about her lips vanished. 'I wasn't being serious!' She watched his brows lift in response to the horrified vehemence of her tone and added, 'And even if I did want to sightsee, by the time I check my emails my dad will have found me one or two things to do,' she promised, flashing a wry smile.

'Then don't check your emails.'

The simple logic made Megan blink as she stared at him as though he were from another planet. 'You might be your own boss, but I'm not. My dad does not have a great opinion of slackers.'

'And are you a slacker?' he wondered, making his interest sound academic.

Megan's response was not academic, it was indignant. 'I am not!'

One corner of his mouth lifted and the amusement extended to his dark eyes. 'You are the boss's daughter—that must give you a certain amount of latitude.'

'Being the boss's daughter means I have to prove I can do more than paint my nails—' She turned her head, a suspicious frown forming on her smooth brow. 'Are you trying to wind me up?'

His grin flashed. 'Yes, the ruffled-feather look suits you.' His eyes dropped to her emotionally heaving bosom. 'Realistically, Armstrong isn't going sack you to prove his egalitarian credentials, is he?'

'If I didn't pull my weight he might. But...' she gave a shrug and conceded '...probably not.'

'Because you're his daughter.' He raised a brow in response to her laugh and came to a halt as the second set of lights ahead changed. '*Not* because you're his daughter?'

Her eyes connected with the dark-eyed glance that flickered her way. 'While I'm working for him, to some extent he still controls my life.'

A small silence followed this unemotional explanation as Megan considered a situation she had been thinking about a lot of late.

'So if he sacked you he'd lose that power?'

Megan nodded, turning her head his way as she agreed with this analysis. 'Exactly.' It wasn't until her glance flickered his way and she saw his expression that she realised what she was discussing and more importantly with whom!

Her eyes shot saucer-wide as she gave a dismayed croak. Had she gone mad? She kept her own counsel on certain subjects; she had not even confided her recent half-formed plans to her best friend.

'So now you know all about my dysfunctional family—not a very fascinating subject, so do you mind if we change it?'

Emilio, who knew a lot more about her family than she

suspected, watched the rosy glow wash over her fair skin and his expression hardened as his thoughts drifted back to a specific section of his conversation with Philip that he had brooded angrily over long after his friend had made his farewells the previous day.

CHAPTER FIVE

'WHY is the idea of Megan being groomed to take over the company a joke?'

Philip grinned, then stopped. 'You're serious,' he realised.

It was a struggle to contain his impatience in the face of the Englishman's open-mouthed amazement. 'Why would I not be? It is my understanding that your sister is being groomed to take control one day.'

'How would you know that? Unless you have been secretly following her progress.' Philip grinned at his own joke.

'We have a proactive policy with recruitment. We are always on the lookout for the brightest and the best,' Emilio explained.

'You thought of offering Megan a job?' The possibility appeared to render her brother tongue-tied with amazement.

'She is exactly the sort of candidate we target.' Not directly obviously—such preliminary approaches were made through the aegis of an agency.

'Megan! *Our* Megan?'

'She did graduate top of her class.' Had any of her family actually noticed?

If they had it would be the first time. A quiet member

in a family of large and noisy personalities, Megan had perfected the art of fading into the background to such a degree that she seemed startled when someone actually noticed her.

Emilio had felt his anger rise as he recalled how pathetically grateful she'd been when she had been included by her family.

'Megan always was a bit of a swot,' Philip recalled with an affectionate grin.

'The same has been said of me, but I would call it focus. It is a quality I find essential in those working for me.'

'So you wanted Megan to… Did she refuse you?'

'I was given to understand through an intermediary that she was not available.'

'Megan being headhunted—that's a tough one to get my head around. She's bright, of course she is…I just never thought…'

'Well, your father must have if he's grooming her—'

'He's not,' Philip cut in.

'How can you be so sure?'

'I know my dad. Oh, he's probably told her that he will— that would be his style,' Philip admitted. 'But let her take over…?' He shook his head. 'No way, never in a million years.'

'Why not?'

'Well, for starters, in case you've forgotten, she's a girl.'

'I had noticed she is a *woman*.'

'Dad can talk the talk when it comes to women in the workplace, but at heart he's a chauvinist.'

'You implied that he would not have been unhappy if Janie had shown an interest.'

'Sure, Janie's always been his favourite, and she's—'

Emilio was taken unawares by the level of anger he

was forced to suppress as he prompted coldly, 'You were saying.'

Maybe he hadn't suppressed it all because Philip looked wary as he responded. 'Dad took Megan in when her mum died, but at the end of the day she was…'

'The maid's daughter.'

'I don't think that way,' Philip protested, flushing. 'But Dad does. And her mum was the *housekeeper* before she got herself pregnant.'

Emilio schooled his expression into neutrality. He had no idea why the sordid story made him so furious. It wasn't as if such things had not occurred in his own family. The only difference being that no member of his family would have ever acknowledged the child of such an unequal union, even if she had been left alone after the death of her mother.

To give Armstrong his due he had recognised his responsibilities even if it had taken twelve years for him to do.

He could only imagine what it had been like for a child brought up in what, according to Philip, had been a pretty tough housing estate in an industrial town to be removed into a totally foreign environment among people she did not know.

People who did not value the gift they had been given.

Megan's glance moved from his long fingers drumming an impatient tattoo on the steering wheel to his profile. The taut lines of his face suggested Emilio wasn't very happy, the tension was rolling off him in waves.

'I hate driving in heavy traffic too. You can't wonder that road rage happens.'

Her soft contralto voice dragged Emilio free of his dark reflections. He turned his head and felt something squeeze tight in his chest as he read the sympathy in her face and all his submerged protective instincts rose to the surface.

'I do not feel rage towards the road.' Just every person who has ever hurt you. 'But you still carry on working for him?'

The abrupt and seemingly unconnected angry addition made her start slightly and blink in confusion.

'Dad?'

He nodded abruptly.

'Why wouldn't I?' No longer an impression—the anger he was projecting was very real.

'So you don't mind that by your own admission he tries to manipulate you.'

'Manipulate is a strong word,' she retorted with manufactured optimism in face of his bewildering level of disapproval.

Not strong enough in Emilio's view for a father who had no interest in his daughter's potential being fulfilled, just her usefulness to him. Did she realise that he had no intention of ever letting go of the golden carrot he dangled?

'If he will not sack you, why worry?' More to the point, why carry on working for the guy?

'There are worse things than being sacked,' she retorted.

'Such as?' he asked, reminding himself that what went on between Armstrong and his daughter was none of his business.

'What is this—twenty questions?' she asked crankily. 'If you must know he'll make an example of me.' She could hear him now: *Just because you're my daughter, Megan.* 'Something suitably humiliating, a public dressing-down, a demotion, at least on paper.'

Her job description and salary might change, but Megan,

who knew despite her father's complaints that she was good at what she did, doubted her workload would alter.

'But as I'm going to be a good girl and refuse your very *tempting* offer of breakfast,' she said, masking the disturbing truth with sarcasm, 'it's kind of academic. And don't pretend to be disappointed. Admit it—you can think of better ways to spend your days than showing me around the tourist sights.'

'I can think of better ways to spend my day,' he admitted, looking at her lips and thinking about several of them; all involved a bed and none featured clothes.

She had never imagined any different, so the anticlimax she felt at his admission was totally irrational.

The lights changed and, while Megan was considering the subtle but important difference between brutal honesty and plain bad manners, Emilio drew away.

At least he had finally dropped the subject. Megan was gazing out through the passenger window, beginning to loosen up slightly when he said something that tipped her over into heart-racing panic…as she found it preferable to designate the erratic thud of her heart as it climbed its way into her throat.

'And are you always a good girl, Megan?'

It could have been an innocent question, but not when it was delivered in a throaty drawl that came direct from an erotic fantasy. Not hers—she didn't do fantasies, erotic or otherwise. She was a girl very founded in reality—a girl who right now was shaking.

Did he like his girls bad?

It was bad she had thought the question; at least she had not said it.

She stared at him feeling as though she had slipped into some sort of trance. This conversation, the entire morning, it was all so surreal. She inhaled deeply, getting an unsettling dose of the male fragrance he used along with the sustaining oxygen. God, Megan, get a grip, girl, or failing that get out of this car!

'Always,' she confirmed in a cold little voice—shame about the tremor.

A disturbing smile tugged the corners of his mobile mouth as his glance dropped to the hands clenched in her lap. 'Good girls don't bite their fingernails.'

Unable to stop herself, she slid her hands under her thighs to hide the shameful condition of her fingernails. 'I don't…' She bit off the futile denial and lifted her chin, turning her defiant golden stare on the hands curved lightly around the steering wheel.

Strong hands, hands that were good to look at, much like the rest of him, she suspected. Her amber eyes were glazing as she stared fixedly at his long, tapering brown fingers and nails that were, of course, not bitten, but neatly trimmed. In her head she saw those long brown fingers, dark as they slid over pale flesh.

She clenched her jaw and pushed the image away.

'I bite my nails—so what? I suppose *you* think that it's an external manifestation of some sort of unresolved conflict. Well, think again—it's just a habit.' And one that Megan now intended to cure herself of for good. She had intended to before, but this time she *really* would.

'I just thought you might be hungry,' he returned mildly.

'I'm always hungry,' she admitted without thinking.

The wistful note in her voice drew a smile from Emilio. 'Then that settles it.'

His response drew Megan's attention to his face. 'Settles what?'

'I don't recall you being this belligerent. Low sugar levels?'

The confident assertion drew a snort from Megan. 'There's nothing wrong with my sugar levels.' It was a great pity the same could not be said of her hormone levels, which had been running riotously out of control since Emilio had appeared.

Since he'd kissed her.

The memory she had tried so hard to suppress rushed over her. It was like walking headlong into a solid wall of heat. It stole her breath, her skin prickled hotly, low in her pelvis things tightened. Megan shuddered, her eyes darkening as she remembered the moment his tongue had stabbed deep into her mouth, the abrasive contact making her melt.

Eyes glazed and misty, she half lifted a hand to her lips, then, catching his dark stare, let it fall away.

She took some comfort from the realisation that she was not likely to be the only female whom he had this effect on.

Don't start thinking you're anything special, Megan. You're creased, cranky and the last person in the world he wants to be lumbered with.

So why didn't he dump you in an airport hotel?

She was too warm in her linen jacket, air conditioning or not. Her covetous gaze moved resentfully up from his gleaming shoes. She had not got very far before her resentment fell away, and the emotion that replaced it tightened like a fist in her chest—she might not be special, but Emilio was!

There was a ribbon of colour across his cheekbones accenting the sharp, sybaritic curve as their stares briefly connected.

The challenge in his made her heart beat faster as she let her lashes fall in a protective mesh over her eyes.

'All right, you can buy me breakfast, but nowhere too

posh. I look scruffy.' What could be the harm eating in a public place? And it might be nice to see a part of Madrid that was not her hotel room.

'I had thought we'd go Dutch, but…'

Despite herself, Megan found herself laughing.

CHAPTER SIX

MEGAN lagged a little behind as she followed Emilio into the building. They had crossed the foyer and entered a lift before her preoccupied brain made a fairly obvious leap.

'This is not a restaurant.'

As she spoke the glass doors closed with a silent swish and the elevator rose silently. Megan, who was not fond of heights, did not take the opportunity to look down into the greenery-filled atrium below.

'Smart and beautiful.'

Very beautiful, but not obvious, he mused, studying her face. She had classic English-rose beauty, her face a perfect heart shape, her pale complexion flawless. It was the sort of face that might not leap out of a crowd, but great, actually *fantastic*, bones and once you started looking you found you couldn't stop.

Or is that just me?

She was about as far removed from the plastic production-line beauty that most of the females he encountered boasted, but then she had what cosmetic enhancement and beauticians could not give. Megan had class; quiet, understated class.

Unaware of his scrutiny, Megan slung him a dark look, smoothed her hair and tried to slow her rapid, shallow, audible inhalations as the elevator came to a smooth halt.

She was uneasily aware that vertigo only explained part of her breathing difficulties.

'Annoying and sarcastic,' she countered, directing what she hoped was a cool, calm look up at him. 'What is this place, Emilio?' And why wasn't the damned door opening? she wondered, sliding a stressed look at the button on the wall behind him.

She wasn't claustrophobic and the space was far from cramped, but if the door didn't open soon she wasn't sure how long she could resist the strong impulse that was telling her to push him out of the way and punch in the instruction necessary herself or, failing that, bang on the door for help.

Emilio continued to stare as he gave a shrug of disinterest. The building, situated in one of Madrid's most exclusive residential areas, had been an investment, one that he had actually forgotten he had made until his ever-efficient PA had pointed out that the penthouse apartment being empty could be an obvious solution to his temporary housing situation.

'I live here.'

Megan's stomach went into a lurching dive as she digested this information in silence. *'Live?'* She was able to keep the panic from her voice, but not her tawny eyes, as she stared at a point midway up his broad chest. 'Live as in...?'

He looked amused by the question. 'Live, as in I go home to at the end of the day.'

Her eyes dropped as the sarcasm in his voice brought a flush to her cheeks. Agreeing to eat with him in a public place with people around was one thing, but this was not what she'd signed up for!

For God's sake, Megan, she counselled herself crossly,

act your age. How long could it take to swallow a cup of coffee and gulp down a pastry?

What was the alternative, run away like a frightened kid?

Emilio Rios, she reminded herself, could literally have any woman he wanted. He's not lured you to his apartment to make a pass at you!

The recognition *should* have made her feel happier.

It didn't. It wasn't that she wanted to be someone else, she was happy being herself, but it would have been nice to know what it felt like to exude that indefinable something that made men notice you *that way*.

Men?

Or was it one specific man she wanted to notice her?

Megan closed down the line of thought, drawing a firm line under the ludicrous flow of speculation. She was a practical person, not given to wishing for things she could not have, and no amount of wishful thinking or Chanel suits were going to give her what women like Rosanna were born with.

As for wanting to be *noticed* by Emilio Rios… She pressed a hand to her stomach where a fluttering had joined the hollow feeling; even the *thought* of such a thing made her feel queasy.

Or something!

'We could go to a restaurant if you prefer?'

Megan found herself responding to the challenge, imagined or otherwise, in his voice.

'No, this is fine.' She glanced down at her watch, silently trying to calculate how soon she could make an escape without looking rude.

Five minutes tops to gulp down coffee and a pastry, Megan reckoned, though actually what was so bad about appearing rude? It wasn't as if he would recognise polite conversation if it bit him on his bottom.

'You're not on the clock. Relax.'

'I am relaxed,' she gritted, plastering on a determined smile.

Emilio, who had seen nervous bridegrooms who looked more relaxed, did not comment. 'You seemed surprised that I have an apartment. What did you think—I sleep at my desk?' he asked, sounding amused.

Her golden eyes swept upwards. 'Wherever you sleep, I'm sure it's not alone.'

'And that bothers you?' He framed the question slowly, his perceptive gaze trained on her face.

Megan found his expression unreadable, but she couldn't shake the crazy conviction he could read her mind.

'Bother?' Her slender shoulders lifted in an uninterested shrug. 'It's none of my business what you do or with whom.'

'But I'm guessing that doesn't stop you having strong views on the subject,' he drawled ironically.

'I have none whatsoever,' she retorted without a blush.

She was just glad that there was no Josh to challenge her lie.

She hadn't even realised that she zeroed in on every reference to Emilio she came across until her flatmate Josh had pointed it out after she had had delivered a few juicy quotes from an offending article, and then, despite his clear lack of interest in the subject matter, had thrust it under his nose.

'How does her dress stay up? That's what I'd like to know.'

It was clear from the red-carpet shot of the couple that Emilio knew how it came off. The woman was plastered up against him like glue.

'Mioaw!' Josh laid the paper aside without looking at it and carried on drinking his coffee. 'Why the interest in this guy, Megan?'

'I'm not interested.'

He arched a brow. 'And judgemental, which isn't like you.'

'I'm not—' Innately honest, Megan was unable to complete the sentence. 'Well, Emilio can be pretty judgemental himself.' And with an awful lot less cause! She recalled his lecture on the last occasion they had met, despite the fact that she had been the victim of an unwanted pass and he had treated her like some sort of tart.

'Really? That sounds interesting.'

'Well, it wasn't,' she said discouragingly. She had no intention of dredging up the humiliating subject for Josh or, for that matter, anyone else.

She had put it very firmly behind her.

'He is just a friend of Philip's.'

'For someone who's not interested you seem awfully concerned about who he's sleeping with.' Josh, his blue eyes gleaming, angled a speculative look at her flushed face. 'Were you two ever…?'

'No, we were not!'

Chuckling, Josh held up his hands. 'I just thought maybe he was the man.'

'What man?'

'The one responsible for your nun-like existence.'

'I have a healthy social life—'

Josh cut across her protest. 'And zero sex life, and don't try and deny it, sweetheart, the walls are extremely thin. You could no more have a secret affair than I could.'

Knowing a defensive comment would prolong the teasing, she had maintained a dignified silence, but it had started her thinking.

Perhaps she did think a little too much about Emilio Rios?

He was not even part of her life any longer. He had been a friend of Philip's, not hers, so there was no reason for him to contact her. They lived in very different worlds.

Pushing away the memory of that embarrassing conversation, she looked Emilio in the eyes and added, 'But I'd sooner not read about it while I'm eating my breakfast.' She pursed her lips primly. Tales of a person's sexual stamina were not, in her opinion, suitable reading for any time of day.

Emilio arched a brow as he wedged his broad shoulders up against the glass wall of the elevator as he studied the top of her glossy head.

The urge to run his fingers across the smooth conker-brown surface and allow the glossy strands to slide through his fingers was almost impossible to resist.

Megan had renewed her study of the carpeting.

She mightn't have strong views on whom he slept with, but he was certainly bothered by whom she spent her nights with, he conceded wryly. If Philip was right about the boyfriend moving out—and Emilio did not think that was an unreasonable conclusion to draw from his comment that *Megan was thinking of moving as her present place was too expensive now Josh had moved out*—it seemed hopeful that this Josh was no longer one of that number.

Having managed to remain blasé while convincing him she cared not at all about whom he slept with or where, Megan felt the colour rush to her face the moment their eyes connected.

'Do you live alone?' You just carry on digging that hole, Megan! And why not jump in for good measure?

'I do. How about you?' he asked casually.

'Yes, I do.' Megan cleared her throat and added, 'I was wondering, is there a problem with the lift?'

It was actually pretty hard to sound casual when you were trying not to inhale his scent—not scent in a perfume sense. Although soap and shampoo were definitely involved, mingled in there with the more disturbing fragrance was a scent of warm male and Emilio.

She forced a breath into her oxygen-deprived lungs and shuddered with the effort.

'Are you all right?'

The mocking light had faded from Emilio's eyes as, concern etched in the furrows on his broad brow, he took a step towards her. Her skin was as pale as paper, the only trace of colour remaining in her face the rich tawny gold of her wide-spaced eyes.

Megan shadowed the action, her own hasty step backwards bringing her shoulder blades up against the wall of the elevator.

Her reaction sent Emilio's dark brows in the direction of his ebony hairline as he raised both hands to his chest, palm flat out to her. 'Relax. What on earth did you think I was going to do?' he asked, his lean face taut with impatience.

Relax—wasn't bad advice to take if she didn't want to give the impression she was a raving lunatic.

Embarrassed, she peeled herself away from the wall. 'You startled me,' she retorted, a defensive note of complaint in her voice.

'Clearly. I have seen rabbits less jumpy than you.' His eyes narrowed to speculative slits as he slowly scanned her face. 'Anyone would think you are scared of me.'

The velvety rasp in his deep voice had a tactile quality like raw silk. She had no control over the shudder that slid the length of her spine like the stroke of a finger. In her mind the phantom finger was long and tanned and— Stop it, Megan!

Ashamed and exasperated by her escalating physical reaction to every aspect of him, Megan studiously avoided making eye contact as she gritted her teeth.

'*Scared?*' She lifted her chin and laughed at the suggestion. 'I'm sure you make grown men cry, but not me,' she conceded. 'But—' She stopped. He had made her cry, but only the once.

Refusing to allow her thoughts to slip back to an occasion that rated pretty high in her 'the worst moment in my life' league, she sketched a tight smile and added, 'Not today anyway.'

And never again. She would never again allow him to make her feel sordid and grubby.

Emilio looked at her mouth and felt the desire in his veins burn hotter as he thought to himself today would not be soon enough for him.

He had always prided himself on his ability to keep his libido on a leash. There had only ever been one woman who had breached his defences and she was standing here now, standing here wanting him as much as he did her, so he was damned if he was going to deprive himself of the unspoken invitation that glowed in her incredible golden eyes when she looked at him.

A nerve clenched in his cheek as his mask of composure threatened to slip. The scorching sexual tension between them was stronger than anything Emilio had ever experienced in his life—she *had* to be feeling it!

Or was he projecting his fantasies onto her?

The question surfaced and was immediately quashed. He exhaled. He knew when a woman wanted him; she *was* feeling it.

Megan wanted him.

The question he ought to be asking, he told himself, was

why, given the overwhelming, almost primal attraction between them, was she putting on this ludicrous act?

Did she think she could pretend that it wasn't happening and it would go away? Why would she want it to?

He dug his fingers into his close-cropped hair and tried to think past the sexual frustration pounding in his skull and other parts of his anatomy.

The Megan he knew had an engaging candour and here she was acting like some shy virgin, which he knew she wasn't.

A girl who looked like Megan did not go through college without drawing a lot of male attention. In retrospect he could see that it should not have been a surprise to him when her flat door was opened by a half-naked man with a quiz-show-host smile—he turned out to be a doctor—and eyes that were too close together.

And yet it had been a surprise. It had been a total bombshell! Emilio had felt as though someone had just gut-punched him, but of course *someone* hadn't, the humiliation had been totally self-inflicted.

A child could have predicted this, but he hadn't. He had spent a year anticipating this moment, covering, or so he'd thought, every angle, but not once during that time had he thought she would be with someone else.

The guy, clearly very much at home, had invited him in, explaining Megan was in the shower.

Emilio had declined the offer.

Could this be simply out-of-control hormones? Megan lifted a hand to her buzzing head. Maybe he was right—maybe her sugar levels were low. It was better than the alternative—better than admitting that she had zero defences against the sizzling sexual charge he exuded.

'It…it h-hasn't opened,' she stuttered, staring at the closed door.

She heard him curse, the low savage imprecation loud in the confined space as he banged the heel of his hand on the control panel. 'Why on earth didn't you say that you suffer from claustrophobia?' he demanded, scanning her pale classic profile.

'I don't,' she protested, too slow-witted to accept this perfect excuse to explain her odd behaviour.

'So what's wrong with you?' he asked, scepticism mingled with irritation.

Again Megan's tongue bypassed her brain. 'You—' She stopped, then was inspired. 'I was just surprised you live somewhere like this. I always pictured you living in some sort of ancient mausoleum filled with antiques, a town version of your little place in the country.'

He tipped his dark head in a concessionary nod to the suggestion, and straightened up to his full impressive height as the glass doors of the private elevator silently opened into a very white space. Not that she was actually noticing; she was too busy asking herself why she was here.

Like you don't know?

Ignoring the sarcastic contribution of the snide voice in her head and the hard knot of illicit excitement low in her belly, Megan fought her way through the mind-fogging confusion in her head.

Sexual attraction, Megan told herself, was a kind of insanity, and should be treated as such. Knowing her weakness, she reasoned, gave her a degree of control.

Her tawny eyes were drawn in the direction of the tall, silent figure watching her. The silence stretched.

The invitation had been for breakfast, she reminded herself, and that was why she was here. She wouldn't let anything happen again; she would eat and leave. Sure, he had kissed her in the airport and had appeared not to want to stop, but that had been an act. For Emilio kissing her had not been a big deal.

Only it was to her. It was a very big deal to be kissed by Emilio Rios, but she would have died before she'd confess as much to him.

'You did not look surprised, you looked…' He paused, considering the question and, much to her dismay, her mouth.

Unhappy, not just about the way he was staring, but also the idea of him relentlessly pursuing the question to its conclusion, she rushed to fill the developing silence.

'Oh, all right!' She sighed, lifting her hair off her neck with her hand as she pursed her lips and evinced a show of reluctance before admitting, 'You might have been right. I do need feeding.'

For a split second she thought he was going to push, then to her relief Emilio grinned. His smugness, she decided, struggling to drag her stare from the curve of his sensually full lower lip, was infinitely preferable to him guessing the lustful direction of her thoughts.

'I am always right, and I do possess the sort of home you speak of,' he admitted, stepping through the door into the white apartment.

CHAPTER SEVEN

MEGAN moved to follow Emilio and hesitated, unable to shake the irrational conviction that by stepping over the threshold she would be committing herself to more than breakfast, which she wasn't, but what if he thought…?

What if he had more planned than breakfast? She had no doubt that he took sex as casually as he did kisses.

How was he to know she didn't?

She knew she was here for breakfast, but who was to say he did? He might assume that she knew breakfast was some sort of code for sex.

'We could do the restaurant option if you prefer. You did say you looked too much of a mess to be seen anywhere…*posh*,' Emilio reminded her. 'I thought you would appreciate the lack of strangers being traumatised by your appearance.' Strangers did not fit in with his plans for the rest of the day, as he pictured her tangled skein of glossy hair spread out on a pillow.

'Traumatised…' she choked. Her flashing golden eyes narrowed in his face. Indignation had carried Megan across the threshold without realising it until the door did the spooky swishy thing behind her, making her jump, and she momentarily transferred her anger to the inanimate object.

'You afraid that being seen in public with a female who

hasn't got her surgically enhanced boobs on show will be bad for your reputation?' she charged scornfully as she glanced downwards, adding, 'What's wrong with the way I look?'

It was a question that Megan almost immediately bitterly regretted issuing.

As his gaze drifted downwards Emilio reined in his lust with difficulty.

She stood there rigidly, her heart pounding against her ribcage, her stomach churning as his dark eyes made a slow, insolent journey from the top of her head to her toes, then at an equally leisurely pace made the return trip.

Emilio swallowed, his head jerking backwards fractionally as he snapped himself clear of the sensual fog.

'You were the one who was unhappy with the way you look.' At his sides he forcibly unclenched his long fingers.

Time, it seemed, had not lessened the strength of the primal emotions that she had shaken loose in him two years ago. He had wanted her then and he still did…

'You didn't have to agree.'

He frowned. 'Don't put words into my mouth,' he said, staring at her lips still swollen from his kiss.

The husky caution brought Megan's gaze helplessly zeroing in on the area under discussion. She felt her anger slip away as a silent sigh lifted her chest as she shook with the memory of his kiss.

The texture of his warm lips as they moved over her mouth, the lust, slammed through her body making her literally rock back on her heels.

She blinked hard to banish the memory, her control worn paper-thin as she nibbled nervously at her full lower lip, unwittingly riveting his attention to the lush curve.

'You want me to tell you you're beautiful?'

Megan flushed. 'Of course not.'

'I would hardly be the first man to tell you this.'

Emilio had never considered himself a possessive man. He had never been guilty of double standards when it came to the subject of any healthy young woman exploring their sexuality.

It turned out that this enlightened attitude only worked when the woman in question was not Megan.

'Sure, I stop traffic on a regular basis. So, why are you living here if you have a palace or something, or is this where you bring your...?' She stopped, the hot colour rushing to her cheeks.

He arched a brow. 'My...?'

'Nothing.'

Her mortified mumble drew a grin that lightened some of the tension in his lean face. 'Relax, this is not a love nest. I am temporarily homeless, while the experts sort out a bad case of dry rot. A man needs somewhere to lay his head and this location is not inconvenient,' he explained, watching her expression as she completed a slow three-hundred-and-sixty-degree turn.

'I see, you're slumming it.' Some slum! The place was a bachelor's paradise, loft-style living with modern art on white walls, acres of gleaming chrome, leather and high ceilings.

It said nothing to her about the man who lived there.

'You like it?'

'I'm sure it's every boy's dream to live somewhere like this.' If this place did not boast every techno gadget on the market she would eat her designer handbag—actually, her very good rip-off handbag.

Emilio responded to the smiling put-down with a lazy grin. The place was no fulfilment of a dream, it was a convenience and nothing more.

'I have not been called a boy for some time.'

Megan's superior smile wilted as their glances locked; the breath snagged in her throat.

She was not surprised. There was nothing even vaguely *boyish* about the man standing there. He radiated male arrogance like a force field. He was all man, all hard sinew and muscle. He couldn't have been harder if he'd been hewn out of granite, but he wasn't stone, he was flesh. Warm flesh.

The tight knot of desire low in her belly tightened so viciously that she gasped, looking away to hide the desire she felt must be written all over her face.

Emilio was a walking advertisement for masculinity and raw sex. Why was she thinking about sex, raw or otherwise?

Panic suddenly gripped her. 'I don't know what I'm doing here.' Her head came up in response to the hand on her shoulder.

'Yes, you do, Megan.'

Trapped by his dark compelling stare, she swallowed, her cheeks hot as she said in a small voice, 'You offered me breakfast.' The pause that followed her statement stretched her nerves to the breaking point.

'So I did.'

Relieved that he hadn't suggested her reasons for being here were far less clear-cut or innocent, she tried to resist the pressure of the hand on her shoulder that urged her down into one of the leather upholstered chairs.

'Relax.'

He needed to stop telling her that—how on earth could she relax?

He loosened his silk tie and slid off his jacket, flexing his shoulders as if to alleviate some unseen tension in the muscles of his neck as he flung it on a sofa. Megan watched through the inadequate protective screen of her lashes as the action strained the seams of the white shirt he wore.

Her stomach muscles flipped and tightened another disturbing notch in response to the suggestion of restrained power and the faint shadow of body hair visible through the thin fabric.

Was his skin that same deep burnished gold all over?

An image flashed into her head of her fingers moving across the surface. The illusion was strong, so tactile that she had to remind herself it wasn't real, but the tingle in her fingertips and the surge of liquid heat between her thighs were.

Megan, appalled and ashamed by her sexual awareness of him, sucked in a deep breath as she tried to focus on what he was saying.

'So what's the verdict?'

Flustered and embarrassed that he had caught her mentally undressing him and worse, Megan shook her head and echoed warily, *'Verdict?'*

'On the apartment.'

Megan, barely able to conceal her relief, embraced the far safer subject of the interior design with enthusiasm. 'Oh! Very tasteful,' she said, turning her head and seeing, not the room, but the image in her head of Emilio minus his shirt. 'But I'm not really into the minimalist look,' she admitted. 'Or technology.'

'What are you impressed by?' He arched a brow. 'A man who can cook?'

'You can cook?'

The shock in her voice drew a laugh from Emilio. 'I will let you be the judge of that,' he said, rolling up his sleeves to reveal hair-roughened sinewy forearms.

It was clear that Emilio knew his way around a kitchen. As she watched him Megan found herself wondering how well he knew his way around other places. Was he equally skilful in the bedroom? she wondered, watching as he whipped the eggs he had cracked into a bowl.

Shocked and ashamed at the direction of her thoughts, she lowered her gaze and wondered what was happening to her.

'You don't have to do this, you know. A coffee and a pastry or something would be fine.'

'I know I don't have to do this. I want to do this, and coffee and a pastry?' He snorted scornfully. 'I hope that is not your idea of a meal.'

'I don't have a lot of time for food.'

'You should make time for the important things in life.'

'I used to eat out quite a lot at a little place near where I live, but not so much since Josh—' She gave a sigh. Life was a lot duller and quieter since her flatmate and best friend had decided to do a stint with an aid agency.

Her expression softened as she recalled his embarrassed response when she had said how much she admired his decision to quit his job to work in a Third World country.

Paying his debt to society and easing his conscience, he'd said, before he sat back and drew his fat consultant's pay cheque.

She jumped, startled by the loud clatter that came from the kitchen area.

'Sorry, I dropped it,' Emilio said, putting the stainless-steel implement he had just picked up off the floor into the dishwasher.

A hard light of steely determination shone in his eyes as he began to whip the egg whites. It was his intention that, not only would Megan not smile dreamily when she thought about her ex, she would forget he ever existed!

Megan watched as he beat the hell out of the eggs. The

annoyance on his face seemed pretty out of proportion with the incident to Megan, but then who knew? Maybe he was a bit of a diva in the kitchen.

It was half an hour later when Megan sat back in her seat and gave a sigh as she licked the butter from her fingertips. 'You can cook. That was delicious.'

'It was only eggs.' He dismissed the feather-light creation with a self-deprecating shrug and filled her coffee cup. 'Wait until you try my pasta al fungi porcini, and my clams have received rave reviews.'

The smile faded from Megan's face. 'I'm sure they have.'

His comment was a timely wake-up call.

She'd been in danger of feeling special, but she was sure he made all women feel special. Maybe cooking was a tried and tested part of his seduction technique? Not that Emilio needed to feed a woman to get her into bed, she admitted bleakly.

Emilio studied her expression with a frown. 'What's wrong?'

She shook her head and avoided his eyes. 'Nothing.'

'Do not lie to me, Megan, or yourself.'

'What do you mean by that?' she flared. 'I'm not lying,' she contended stubbornly. 'Thank you for the breakfast, Emilio, but I—'

A whistled sound of irritation escaped his clenched teeth. 'From where I'm sitting you have a problem. I think you're in danger of developing a seriously bad relationship with food. Are you feeling guilty because you have eaten?'

She looked at him and thought, I'm feeling guilty because I can't look at you without thinking of you naked.

'Of course not. I promise you I do not have an eating disorder.'

'Not now maybe,' he conceded. 'But these things can be insidious.'

'Food is just not that important to me.'

'Food is not important to all people,' he conceded, leaning forward as he planted his forearms on the table. 'But you are not one of them. Eating is a sensual pleasure. You take pleasure in food because you are a sensual person. Why deprive yourself of this pleasure to fit some stereotypical image? Why fight nature?

'When it comes to food, the question,' he contended, 'is not what time is it, it is are you hungry?'

Megan glared at him in total exasperation. 'Of course I'm hungry. I'm always hungry!' she yelled.

Didn't the stupid man realise that she was fighting nature that had decided in its infinite wisdom that she should be ten pounds heavier? 'As for eating, when I'm hungry if I ate what I *liked* I'd be...'

Emilio, aware that he had hit a raw nerve or possibly several, turned his chair around, dragged it nearer to hers and straddled it. 'Less cranky?'

'Very funny,' she snapped, unappreciative of his smart retort, a comment that could only be made by a person who had never worried about their weight.

Her eyes skimmed scornfully down his body. Either he had iron discipline or an enviably efficient metabolism.

Even fully clothed it was obvious he didn't carry an ounce of excess flesh on his lean frame. He was all hard muscle and sinew.

The butterfly kicks that fluttered in the pit of her stomach made her hastily avert her gaze.

'Do you think I'm a size ten by accident?'

'I wondered if you had been ill,' he admitted.

Megan's jaw dropped as her head turned back towards him. Her amber eyes sparkled with incredulous wrath as she got to her feet.

'I look ill?' It was always ego-enhancing to be told you looked wrecked by a man who, in her head, had been the standard of physical perfection she measured his entire sex by since she was a teenager.

Emilio grinned. He was not oblivious to the danger in her voice, but he was not a man who thought it a virtue to play it safe.

In his opinion a rush of adrenaline made life more interesting and reminded a man he was alive. His eyes followed the swish of her free hair as it settled in a glossy frame to her heart-shaped face. Actually, now that he thought about it, there had been precious few adrenaline rushes in his life of late.

When was the last time he'd clashed with anyone? When was the last time anyone had openly disagreed with him?

And it wasn't just professionally. Even the women in his life censored out any of the contents he might not like before they spoke, never even considering that he might appreciate the challenge of an opinion other than his own.

'You look a little...*faded*.' His eyes slid to her pink lips and he swallowed. 'Like a crushed rose.'

The odd note in his deep voice brought Megan's frowning regard to his face. 'Rose?' she echoed, fighting off the crazy rush of pleasure.

He nodded. 'One who needed a long cool drink or, in this case, breakfast.'

'You're obsessed by food!' she complained, thinking it was better than what she was obsessed by!

It wasn't even as if she were not a very sexual person;

the contrary was true. It was as if that airport kiss had pressed some off switch to the on position!

'No, that is you,' he countered, watching the play of expressions as they moved across her expressive face. It wasn't just her hair that had slipped, it was her composed mask too.

'I'm not obsessed with food.'

Just your mouth and, for that matter, the rest of you!

Switching off the inner commentary, but not before the guilty colour had rushed to her cheeks, Megan dropped her gaze to her hands clasped in her lap.

What was going on? She didn't have thoughts like this.

'A person,' he came back confidently, 'is only obsessed by what they are deprived of.'

Megan's head came up. 'What do you mean by that? I'm not deprived of anything!' she yelled, her defensive voice bouncing off the high ceiling.

He held up his hands in mock surrender, the sardonic gleam in his dark eyes making her shift uncomfortably in her seat. 'I'm delighted to hear it, though some people might think the lady protests too much?'

Lips pursed, Megan shrugged and did not respond to the gentle taunt. 'I simply show a bit of self-control where food is concerned.'

Self-control… Emilio's sloe-dark eyes drifted towards her mouth. Her lips were bare; he remembered the hint of strawberry in the gloss that he had kissed away. Without adornment they were naturally rose-tinted, and amazingly lush, their softness so inviting he struggled to think past the loud buzz in his head and the stab of desire that sliced through him like a knife.

He lifted his gaze, meeting her eyes through the mesh

of his eyelashes. 'Self-control has its place.' Like in an airport.

The ripple of sensation Emilio's sinfully seductive throaty purr set in motion passed through her entire body from her scalp to her curling toes.

Megan, her eyes melded to his smouldering stare, endured the moment breathing through the nerve-shredding sensation. It passed, but the aching lump lodged like a chunk of broken glass in her throat remained.

'I...' Megan was unable to tear her eyes free of his mesmeric stare, and her voice faded. Her lips continued to move, but nothing emerged but a whispery sigh.

When the sexual tension had been in the background she had been able to pretend it wasn't there. That was no longer possible. In the space of a heartbeat it had become an almost visible presence, humming like a high-voltage charge in the air between them, swallowing up the oxygen so that she struggled to breathe.

'Though sometimes it is good to let go.'

Megan, hand pressed to her throat, struggled to catch her breath. She compressed her lips, angry with him for playing games and herself for being such a sucker for his not very subtle tactics, and there was no way in the world it was accidental. Was this some sort of game for him?

'I really wouldn't know. I don't...'

'What? You never let that lovely hair down and throw caution to the wind? Some men could view a statement like that as a challenge.'

'Certainly I let my hair down, but only with people I trust.'

'You think I would take advantage?' Emilio sighed inwardly. She was right.

The predatory gleam in his dark eyes sent a secret shiver down her spine. 'I'm really not interested in finding out.'

Her declaration of indifference drew a low chuckle from him. The scarily attractive sound made Megan bite the inside of her cheek.

'You are probably…' he mused, studying her with an intent expression that made Megan want to cover her face with her hands.

'Probably what?' she snapped when the dramatic pause stretched beyond bearable limits.

'The worst liar of any woman I have ever met.'

Her eyes flew wide. 'I am a *very* good liar!' she cried, bouncing to her feet.

Megan gave him the evil eye when her unthinking indignant rebuttal drew another throaty chuckle, of the incredibly sexy variety, from him.

'What's that on your mouth?' Emilio asked, no longer looking amused as he got to his feet and reached out towards her face.

Megan reacted to his hand like a striking snake, her heart beating a furious tattoo as she ducked away from his touch.

He raised an eloquent brow in response to her instinctive action as, feeling foolish, Megan slid her eyes from his.

'What's what?' she said, lifting a hand to the corner of her mouth. Her finger came away smeared red. 'Oh, it's nothing,' she said dismissively as she fished a tissue from her pocket.

His dark brows twitched into a disapproving straight line above his hawkish nose. 'It looks more like blood to me.'

Megan rolled her eyes. Talk about overreaction. 'Why are the Spanish so dramatic?' she asked, clicking her tongue in irritation as she added, 'It's a microscopic speck of blood. If you must know, I bit myself,' she admitted, wishing something would distract his attention from her mouth.

To have his dark-eyed scrutiny trained with unblinking intensity on her lips was sending her nervous system into frantic overdrive.

'That was not a clever thing to do,' he mused, leaning in close—too close—and taking the tissue from her hand.

Their fingers brushed before she could take evasive action and then she didn't want to. A shiver wafted across the sensitised surface of her skin making all the downy hairs stand on end.

Her nostrils flared in response to the scent of his body: warm, musky male smell overlaid with the clean scent of the spicy soap he used.

Struggling against the tide of enervating heat that washed through her, Megan, who was sure her struggle was written across her face in neon, did not make the mistake of meeting his eyes.

Instead she trained her eyes on his strong jaw, close enough to see the dark rash of stubble and the faint white scar that angled upwards in the direction of his cheekbone.

'I'm not clever.' The words came out a husky whisper as she thought, No, I'm insane, as in certifiable.

The flash of insight did nothing to halt the growing fluttering sensation of excitement low in her stomach. She caught her lower lip between her teeth, swallowing hard as her covert glance flickered across the strong angles and planes of his incredible face.

'But you are a very good cook.'

'Would you like some more?'

She shook her head. 'If I ate what I wanted when I wanted I'd be ten pounds heavier,' she said honestly. 'And a lot of those pounds would be on my boobs and hips.'

'And that is a problem?'

The anger sizzled up out of nowhere. Her hands

clenched into tight fists, squeezing the blood from her whitened knuckles. She was suddenly so angry she couldn't breathe.

'Yes, as men appear to measure a woman's availability and her morals by the size of her breasts!' she yelled, pressing her hands flat on her heaving C-cup bosom, still able to see Emilio's expression when she had turned to him with tearful gratitude, thanking him for saving her.

CHAPTER EIGHT

Two years had passed, but Megan could recall the entire scene in painful, mortifying, word-perfect detail that time had not dulled—if anything time had intensified the humiliation.

Ironic, really—if Emilio hadn't arrived when he had, if instead she had been able to extricate herself from the situation with a few of the dirty tricks that her brother had said no girl should be without, the incident might now have faded to a memory. Maybe she'd even have been able to smile at it.

But the memory hadn't faded. Instead it had grown in her mind out of all proportion. It had lost none of its ability to tie her stomach into nauseous knots because Emilio *had* walked in, or, rather, past the parked car. He had flung open the car door with a force that had almost wrenched it from its hinges.

Megan's initial relief had rapidly morphed into shock mingled with dismayed confusion as she'd registered the expression on Emilio's lean face. In Megan's mind her brother's handsome Spanish friend with his excitingly different background and charming accent had always epitomised urbane, sophisticated charm.

The golden skin drawn tight across the strong bones of his face, raw, brutal fury etched into every plane and angle of the hard lines of his patrician visage, the man with the blazing dark eyes had seemed like a stranger.

He had responded to her escort's drunken slurred protests with a storm of staccato Spanish before he had literally dragged the man from the car and vanished into the trees with him.

Megan never knew what happened during the five minutes Emilio was gone. But next time their paths had crossed at the university her lecturer had forgotten the ultra-cool image he liked to cultivate and run, gown flapping, in the opposite direction like a scared rabbit.

When Emilio had returned she had already got out of the car and had been relieved to see the explosive fury had vanished. He seemed calm, cold even.

She had gathered her courage in both hands and levelled a wary look at his face, still able to remember his anger, still seeing a stranger when she looked at him. But her dignified thank-you had been genuine, even though she had wished it had been anyone else but Emilio who had rescued her from the mortifying situation.

'Did you *want* saving?'

The response bewildered her until she saw his expression.

The scorn and aristocratic disdain etched on his patrician features made her cringe. She felt crushed by his scorn. It was bad enough that the man she had had a secret crush on since she was a kid had witnessed the grubby sordid scene, but that he could think she had *wanted*... If she could have crawled out of her skin at that moment Megan would have. She stuttered in her eagerness to correct him.

'No...no, that is, yes, you can't think that I wanted... Of course I—'

'You were a fool.'

Unable to deny the scathing denouncement, she shook her head and blinked back tears. Did he think she didn't know that? Did he think she needed it rubbed in?

As she stood there she silently prayed for the ground to open up and swallow her—maybe even out loud; that part remained a little vague. But it didn't so she simply had to stand and endure the contemptuous study, nailed to the spot with scorching humiliation, mortified beyond belief as the sweep of his disparaging stare moved from the top of her glossy head to her feet shod in a pair of high-heeled ankle boots.

'You say you didn't want anything, but appearances suggest otherwise. You look like you've been poured into that top, and as for the jeans...'

Megan dragged down at the rounded high neckline of the shirt she wore today under her business suit, closing her eyes as she still recalled the condemnatory glow in his eyes as his sweeping gesture had encompassed the V-necked black T-shirt—black because she'd thought the colour was slimming—before sliding to the dark denim jeans, the brand and style that all her friends had been wearing without being accused of flaunting anything.

'What reaction did you expect?' Megan heard him ask as she focused her attention, not on the condemnation in his eyes, but the nerve in his lean cheek that was clenching and unclenching.

He stabbed his long fingers into the dark waves of his thick hair and released a string of expletives in Spanish, sounding and looking nothing like the quietly authoritative man who had always been kind to her and, even more amazingly, appeared interested in what she was doing, possibly because he had lovely manners.

'As for getting into a car with a boy who had been drinking...'

His sneering disdain made her see red. 'He's not a boy, he's a lecturer.'

'Do the university authorities look kindly on their lecturing staff dating their students?'

'It wasn't a date, he was just—'

'I saw what he was just doing, and if you choose to have casual sex it might be a good idea to remember that drunks have a very slender grasp of safe sex!'

The accusation horrified Megan. 'He wasn't—'

'Are you saying he had not been drinking?'

'No, I'm...' She shook her head, struggling to equate this cold, cruel critic with the person who had always had a kind word of encouragement for her in the past.

Her miserable silence seemed to incense him further.

'Have you been drinking also?' he asked, his hooded gaze suspicious as he studied her face.

At that point a small burst of defiance, long overdue it seemed in retrospect, came to Megan's aid.

Planting her hands on the curve of her hips, she thrust out her chin, tossed back her hair. 'If I wanted to have a drink, so what?' she challenged, her voice husky as she forced the words past the aching emotional lump in her throat.

'It's not illegal, you know. I'm over eighteen.'

'This is not about *legality*, it is about self-respect.'

Megan, unable to stand there and take the sheer breathtaking unfairness of the cutting condemnation, choked back a sob and yelled, 'I wasn't attending an orgy! It was just a few friends, a university thing... Actually, it's none of your business. You're not my father.'

Inexplicably, or so it seemed to Megan, he took her response as a tacit admission of guilt.

'So you have!' His eyes closed, he let his head fall back, exposing the long line of his brown muscled throat as he inhaled deeply, then slid apparently unwittingly into his native tongue, ending the tirade with a biting, *'Well?'*

Well, what? she thought. 'I had one glass of wine,' she admitted after a fulminating silence. 'I said I'd get a taxi, but he offered—'

'How did you expect the man to react when you look like that? It's an open invitation to…to…' The rest of the insult was delivered once more in his native tongue, but this time a crushed Megan definitely got the gist!

'I said no.'

'Clearly not loudly enough. He said…'

'What did he say?'

'He said you were gagging for it.'

Megan, white-faced, pushed away the images crowded into her head and refocused on the present.

'I prefer to steer clear of the D-cup she's-gagging-for-it look.' As she spoke she saw the flash of shocked recognition in his eyes and wished the words unsaid.

Her intention had always been, should he ever refer to the subject—admittedly unlikely—to shrug it away as though she barely recalled it. The last thing she wanted was Emilio to guess what sort of indelible impression the incident had had on her.

'You are speaking of that night when that little loser made a pass.'

His retrospective take on the evening drew a laugh from Megan. 'You mean that innocent victim I led on?' She bit her lip and thought, Could you sound any more bitter, Megan?

A nerve clenched in his lean cheek.

If it had been anyone else she would have interpreted the look that flashed across his face as discomfiture, but this was Emilio Rios, who did not know the meaning of awkward.

He dragged a hand down his jaw and expelled an irritated-sounding sigh. 'I was angry that night.' He had been angry that entire weekend, from the moment she had walked into the room the previous evening smelling like summer and looking like warm, inviting sin, looking as if she were made for him.

The forced admission made her laugh. 'I'd never have guessed.'

Even now the memory of his loss of control shook Emilio. He had never before or since come closer to totally losing it. The red haze had consumed him totally.

'The situation was…'

She angled an interrogative brow as his voice trailed away to a growl.

'I did not handle the situation well.'

As apologies went it was pretty feeble. 'Being my brother's mate did not make you the guardian of my morals and you had no right to judge me!'

'I did not judge you. I was trying to protect you, Megan.'

'You made me feel grubby.' She saw the flash of shock in his eyes and dropped her gaze.

'That was not my intention.'

Not his intention, but the result nonetheless. 'It doesn't matter. It was a long time ago.'

'Not so long ago and it clearly does matter,' he said, feeling intense guilt as he studied her face.

'Look, let the subject drop. Like I said, it was a long time ago.'

'My actions were…not acceptable.'

He had been more out of control than he had ever been at any other time in his life.

When the guy had bleated out the clichéd defence and even tried to suggest Megan had not meant no, Emilio had come closer than he even liked to admit to himself to choking the life out of the sleaze.

It had not occurred to him until now that he had vented his frustration on Megan. Frustration that had been building the entire weekend. When he had come back and seen her standing there, the tears on her cheeks, her hair tangled and her mouth bruised from another man's kisses, all that frustrated sexual hunger and guilt he had been keeping under tight control for the entire weekend had exploded.

'And then some.' His remorse seemed genuine, but Megan was not prepared to let him off the hook just yet. 'I think, Megan, that you—'

She held up her hand. 'Don't bother, I know what you think about me. You made yourself quite clear at the time, practically telling me I was a little tart who was a danger to the moral well-being of the entire male population for a hundred-mile radius.'

'Don't be ridiculous. I didn't say anything like that.' Their eyes connected and he shrugged, admitting, 'All right, I might have given that impression, but that was only because...'

'Because you were disgusted by my *slutty* clothes. Well, as a matter of fact, they weren't. They were perfectly ordinary things for—'

'Jeans, very tight, and the clingy black top. It kept slipping off your shoulder—your bra strap was pink,' he recited. His dark eyes drifted towards her mouth as he continued to catalogue. 'Your lipstick was pink too. It was smeared.' He swallowed convulsively before adding in the same flat, colourless tone, 'And your lip was bleeding.'

Until he'd seen the blood he had been holding it together quite well. All right, not *well* as such, but he had been keeping his more primitive instincts in check. But those tiny beads of red on her skin had made something snap inside him.

Megan's jaw dropped. 'You still remember.' And in detail. Even she didn't remember what colour her lipstick had been that night. Her ensemble appeared to have been so truly awful that it had imprinted itself on the memory of a man who had perfect taste.

Actually he had perfect everything, she thought, concentrating on her resentment that rose in direct proportion to the perfection, rather than the liquid rush of excitement low in her belly.

Her legs were jelly, inside her bra her breasts chafed painfully against the lace. Stop acting like you don't have a choice, she told herself. There's always a choice.

Her moment of rebellion lasted as long as it took for her gaze to wander back to his mouth.

She struggled against a wave of lust. It was insane, she thought, running the tip of her tongue across the curve of her dry lips, but when it came to being a total pushover that theoretical choice was just that—theoretical.

The way Emilio made her feel was one thing in her life that she had no choice about!

She was stuck with loving the way he looked. Loving the way he sounded, the way he smelt, the way he moved… Actually love was perhaps the wrong word to accurately convey the visceral intensity and power of the effect he had on her.

On the other hand, maybe *love* was exactly the right word.

Megan's pupils dilated with shocked rejection as she pushed away the dangerous thought and narrowed her wandering focus to one little triangle of olive-toned tanned skin at the base of his throat. Even that tiny section of skin set in motion a stream of erotic conjecture.

This was so unfair. What chance did she have? Linen didn't dare crease on him. In a fair world it ought to be illegal for any man to be this good-looking.

Conscious that the silence had lengthened, she dragged her thoughts away from the steamy place they were in danger of returning to and angled a hostile stare up at his face.

'Have you got a photographic memory or something?' Was the embarrassing moment never going to be allowed to die?

'No, I do not, but I have excellent recall for some things.' The weekend he had realised that he had been a blind fool had lingered in his mind.

'I didn't look *that* bad. Did I?' She bit her lip, hating the fact she sounded as if she was asking for his approval.

And you're not?

The question made him blink. '*Bad...?*' Emilio ejaculated hoarsely.

He shook his head. The rest of the world looked at Megan and saw an incredibly beautiful woman, but what, he wondered grimly, did she see when she looked in the mirror?

Had that boyfriend of hers been too busy admiring himself in the mirror to make her see she was stunning? His opinion of the man, never high, now zoomed to below zero. As for that family of hers, he brooded darkly, they had a hell of a lot to answer for!

On his visits to the Armstrong household over the span of several years, Emilio had been forced on numerous occasions to remind himself it was not his business as he watched the attempts of Philip's little sister, not to win approval or praise from her family, but simply to be noticed.

Doomed attempts, obviously it went without saying.

The Armstrongs were a loud, egocentric bunch too busy with their own lives to show any interest in anything else, especially the new and painfully unsure member of the family.

'There's no need to yell,' Megan bellowed, then looked shocked. She was not in the habit of raising her voice, as much as the last hour belied that fact.

From the expression on his dark face she had the strong feeling that Emilio was equally unaccustomed to being yelled at.

On another occasion his astounded expression might have amused her, but at that moment she felt as though she might never laugh again.

Emilio swore under his breath, the muscles along his strong jaw tightening as his scorching dark gaze swept across the features turned up to him. Being furious with her was not reducing the level of his painful arousal. If anything it was feeding the desire that licked through his veins like a forest fire, out of control—did he want to control it?

Emilio shifted his weight in a futile effort to ease the pain in his groin. This was not a moment for deep analysis. He could barely string a sequence of intelligible words together, let alone indulge in self-analysis of the complex mixture of emotions that he was struggling with.

Megan, her head tilted to one side, watched through the veil of her lashes as he dragged a shapely brown hand through the ebony strands of his gleaming dark head. Her level of fascination with his fingers, the size, elegance, strength and shape of his hands, was beginning to escape her control.

What control? asked the ironic inner voice in her head.

'*Por Dios*, there is every need to shout,' he contended,

studying her flushed face with an air of scowling disbelief as he fought to subdue the protective feelings that surfaced when he saw the reflection of whatever inner battle she was fighting shining in her eyes.

It was easier to focus on his anger.

He *knew* she was feeling the erotic charge that hung heavily in the air between them. How could she not? It almost had a physical presence.

Why was she fighting it? Why couldn't she just relax and let it happen? His jaw clenched in frustration. It was as if she couldn't get past the fact he'd been the one to rescue her from an unpleasant and potentially dangerous situation.

Was it because he'd seen her vulnerable? Did that not mesh with the cool, controlled image she obviously wanted to project?

He dragged a hand down his jaw and decided it was useless to try and figure out her reasoning because, quite clearly, there was none.

CHAPTER NINE

'Was I drunk?'

The simmering hostility in Emilio's manner as much as the abrupt question made Megan blink. 'What?'

His dark eyes flashed. 'Was I forcing myself on you? *Por Dios*, no, I was not!'

'I never—'

'So at what point did I become the bad guy?' he demanded, cutting across her.

'I never—'

'The fact is you were lucky I was there, but you're too stubborn to admit it! You are just as stupid now as you were then!'

Megan's chin went up at the insult. Eyes narrowed, she threw back her head, glaring up at him with simmering hostility. 'And you are just as arrogant and judgemental.'

A hissing sound of irritation escaped his clenched teeth. 'Also, do you know,' he drawled, 'how incredibly boring this ugly-duckling routine of yours is?'

Megan's amber eyes lit up like beacons with anger. 'Oh, I'm *so* sorry to bore you.' If she'd been some long-legged lissom beauty with plastic boobs attached to a skeletal clothes-hanger frame he would no doubt make allowances for an IQ in single figures.

Emilio's teeth audibly ground in response to her sarcastic insincerity.

'Of course, if I had known I was expected to *entertain* you, I'd have made more of an effort—worn a funny nose, perhaps?' she suggested, pressing the tip of her finger to her small, classically perfect nose.

He gave a hard laugh and watched as her hand fell, revealing the delicate purity of her features only spoiled from being textbook classical by the generosity of her lips. Emilio, his eyes glued to the full, lush curve, did not think it spoiled anything.

It took every ounce of his strength not to grab her and crush her mouth under his. He inhaled sharply through flared nostrils and snarled.

'Do not be absurd!'

His dismissive, plain nasty attitude fed her anger and sense of growing resentment. 'So I'm assuming for "absurd" read anyone who says anything you don't like?'

Which couldn't, she reasoned darkly, be something that happened very often. The problem with Emilio Rios was that people were willing to cross oceans, let alone roads, to avoid antagonising him, and from where she was standing it was easy to see why.

He had not gained the reputation of being a bad man to get on the wrong side of by accident! And he did look pretty magnificent if you liked your dark and moody with an edge of danger.

And she, it turned out, did!

As Megan watched a shaft of sunlight from an angled skylight hit his face. He had no reason to fear the unforgiving light; there were no flaws or shortcomings to be revealed.

He was perfect.

A furrow of concentration appeared between Megan's

feathery brows as her rapt gaze lingered on the hard angles and hollows of his patrician face, the strong, sculpted contours emphasised by the dusting of dark hair sprinkled already over his clean-shaven jaw. She wondered how it would feel against her skin and shivered, unable to tear her rapt gaze from his face.

He was nothing short of breathtaking to look at!

'You make a great deal of effort to be rude to me, *querida*. I wonder why?' he mused.

'It's no effort, believe me, and don't call me that,' she snapped, her discomfort increased by the casual endearment.

Privately she conceded he did have a point. Where was the diplomacy she was famed for? Winding Emilio up was a bit like getting into a tiger's cage and throwing sticks at it.

A person had to expect the tiger to leap so the question remained why? A mental image of Emilio falling across her body flashed into Megan's head, the erotic fantasy so powerful that she could actually feel the weight of his body, the heat of him bearing down on her.

The effort of expelling the erotic intrusion wrenched a soft grunt from her aching throat that drew a quizzical look from Emilio.

Megan decided to avoid tiger analogies for the foreseeable future and took refuge in hostility—*again*.

'What can I say? My job entails being pleasant to men who have to be told at regular intervals how marvellous they are. I'm on my own time.' Her dad might disagree on that detail, but then nothing she had done so far today was going to make him break out in song. 'I don't have to play nice.'

A white line of anger appeared around the sensual outline of his sculpted lips as Emilio drew himself up to his full intimidating height.

'I am not your father,' he snarled, totally incensed by the implied comparison she made with a man he despised.

Megan, aware she had been appallingly indiscreet, not to mention unprofessional, began to back-pedal furiously. 'I didn't mean Dad, just men in a position of power generally,' she finished lamely.

Emilio ignored her protestations. 'And I do not,' he imparted grimly, 'need my ego stroked.'

How about other parts?

Shocked, not just by the shameless question that popped into her head, but the accompanying images that followed the thought, Megan dropped her gaze from his as she felt the shamed colour fly to her cheeks. She was not the sort of girl who went around mentally undressing men.

'It's the effect you have on me,' she mumbled, struggling to find a plus side to this situation. He couldn't read her mind, though sometimes when he looked at her she did get the uncomfortable feeling that she had no secrets from him.

'It was not my intention to…' His voice faded as she began to nibble nervously at her full lower lip.

The silence stretched way beyond dramatic pause and into nerve-shredding territory until finally Megan could bear it no longer.

'Not your intention to what?'

Her voice dragged Emilio from the hot place his thoughts had gone. He blinked and met her eyes, still imagining her lips parting to allow his tongue deep inside.

'Not my intention to—' He paused again and exhaled slowly.

He could have said lose the thread…lose the plot… Both, to his intense shock, were true. He could sit in a high-powered meeting that went on into the small hours and when others faded, not miss a beat, stay on top of every detail discussed, some buried in a mass of techno babble, yet he looked at Megan's mouth and his brain was mush.

Emilio chose to fast-forward the conversation. 'I find your self-deprecating attitude annoying. You are a beautiful woman and, believe it or not, I was trying to help that night, not judging.'

Megan gave a derisive hoot. 'Sure you weren't.' *Beautiful?* Her stomach muscles did a shimmy as she directed a wary look at his face, waiting for the punchline and telling herself not to start seeing or hearing things that weren't there.

'It was not your clothes that night,' he said abruptly, 'though they were enough to—' He inhaled, turning his hand away sharply, providing Megan with a view of the nerve pulsing in his hollow cheek and the cords of tension standing out in his brown throat.

'Of course, I can see the sense of power you had discovered must have been intoxicating,' he conceded, struggling to be fair-minded and failing big time as he thought of Megan enjoying her feminine power in the arms of men like that creep he had dragged from the car.

As he remembered the fear in the said creep's eyes he smiled thinly, not regretting having put it there—at least he knew there would be one less guy supplying willing arms.

She gave a baffled shake of her head, confused as much by his strained manner as his peculiar choice of words. *'Intoxicating?'*

'You'd pretty much been invisible at home all through your adolescence and, I assume, school.' Recalling the slights and snubs he had witnessed and imagining the ones he had not, Emilio struggled to keep his voice impassive.

'Thanks.' Megan finally saw where he was going with this. It was always good to be told you were a needy and pathetic outsider. 'So you're suggesting at some point I morphed into an equally pathetic attention seeker with self-esteem issues.' She wasn't sure which was worst.

His lips twisted in a spasm of impatience. 'Don't spin my words. I'm *saying* that the tables were turned. You weren't the one doing the vying. It was not surprising that, after years of being overlooked, being the focus of male attention should go to your head. You wouldn't be the first person deprived of parental approval to confuse sex with love. Sex is only ever a short-term fix.'

The expression in his eyes when he drew this bleak conclusion made Megan wonder if this was personal.

Was Emilio thinking of the women he had slept with since his marriage collapsed when he spoke of short-term fixes? Was Rosanna the only woman he had ever loved? It was obvious after the airport debacle that, whatever he said, he was not over her.

'It is hard to recover your self-respect, Megan, once you have lost it.'

'Is that a polite way of saying you think I'm a tart?'

'Do not put words in my mouth,' he responded irritably.

Megan gave a bemused shrug and stared up at him. For a man with the reputation of infallibility, she reflected grimly, when Emilio got it wrong he got it wrong big time!

'And you got all that from the colour of my lipstick! Amazing, you're even smarter than they say.'

The muscles around his jaw tightened at her mock admiration. 'Oh, so I'm meant to believe you didn't have the *faintest* idea what you could do to me...a man, looking that way.'

'Do to a man?' Her eyes widened. The expression

smouldering in his deep-set eyes made her heart kick up several more uncomfortable notches. 'Me? Sure,' she drawled, coating her words with protective cynicism as she batted her eyelashes like crazy and struck a provocative pose, hand on hip. 'It's such a burden being irresistible. Ouch,' she yelled, pulling back as his fingers closed like an iron band around her wrist.

The touch was light and the effect on her nervous system totally disproportionate. 'This habit you have of putting yourself down before someone else does is one you should try to break.'

'I don't—' Emilio watched the flash of recognition in her eyes before they fell from his.

'That hurts,' she lied, wincing not in pain but at the breathy sound of her own voice.

Emilio was breathing hard as he brought her hands together and pressed them, palms sealed, between his.

It was a moment before his gaze lifted from their entwined fingers. The blaze of hunger in his eyes as they connected with her own made Megan's insides dissolve.

'So does wanting a woman so much you can't think of anything else, so much that you can't function!' he growled, jerking her roughly towards him until they stood thigh to thigh.

They were so close now that Megan could hear his heartbeat, or was that her own? His hands had moved to the small of her back, leaving her own trapped between their bodies. She might have struggled to work out where he ended and she started, except he was harder...*much* harder. The muscular thighs she was pressed against had as much give as oak-tree trunks.

Shaking her head to clear the dreamy, light-headed sensation, she forced herself to recognise the abrupt rise in her core temperature for what it was: a hormone rush—God, a hormone avalanche!

She struggled hard to inject a note of humour into her response. 'Your concern for your fellow man does you credit, but I promise to behave and never wear pink lipstick again.'

'I have no concern for them.' Emilio dismissed the mental well-being of one half of the population with an expressive sneer. 'And,' he added, gritting out the words with force, 'I don't want you to behave.'

'You don't?' she whispered.

His glittering eyes held hers. 'Not at all,' he confirmed in a deep smoky voice that sent shivers of anticipation down her spine.

Emilio wanted her to misbehave—with him.

She said it twice in her head and it still didn't seem real. Did she even know how to misbehave in the way he clearly expected? Her eyes drifted to his gorgeous, incredibly sexy mouth and suddenly her lack of experience felt less important as need swelled inside her, tightening into a hard fist of hot desire in her belly.

Emilio was the one man whom she had always been prepared to sacrifice her principles for. She had frequently told herself she was lucky he had never asked her to. That way, she had reasoned, she had no regrets—what she also did not have, but had not previously acknowledged, were no memories.

Now he was standing there, not asking directly but sending some pretty explicit messages, unless she had disastrously misinterpreted his thinly veiled comments and the gleam of sexual intent in his eyes was a figment of her overheated imagination.

She checked. That gleam looked real. It felt real, she

thought as a fresh shiver rippled through her body. At that moment it hit her that it *was* real; she wasn't dreaming.

What am I doing?

Belatedly Megan's self-protective instincts kicked in and her head dropped forward, causing her hair to fall in a silky screen around her face.

Space, she told herself. I need space and I need *not* to say, Take me!

Do not say it, Megan!

She bit down on the shameless words. She remained dumb but couldn't put the space plan into action as her feet remained nailed to the floor.

She felt the sweat trickle down her back and realised with horror that if anything she was leaning into him, not pulling away. Her body just wasn't listening to what her head was telling it.

Her body had its own agenda!

And to make the situation even more unbearable her brain might have closed down but her senses were painfully alert. Being this close to him, being able to smell him, feel the heat coming off his body, was physically painful.

She started shaking like someone with a fever. The intensity of the need pounding through her terrified her. It was utterly and totally outside her experience.

Had he noticed? Of course he had. The knowledge that she was trembling with sheer lust would presumably confirm his conviction she was a bed-hopping tart.

CHAPTER TEN

'WOULD you like to not behave with me?'

This time the invitation left no room for misinterpretation.

Megan felt vulnerable, exposed and excited all at the same time. 'It really isn't that simple.' A person standing on the brink of a precipice stepped back; they did not jump—so why was every atom in her body screaming, Jump?

'It is.' There was no trace of uncertainty in Emilio's voice.

But then why would there be uncertainty in his voice? This was simple for him: he felt an attraction and he acted on it. He had no moral dilemma, no trust issues, no deep fear of having his heart broken.

'Has someone hurt you, Megan?'

His question triggered her self-protective instincts.

'No. There are no great dramas in my life.'

He looked unconvinced by her response, but was quickly distracted. 'Your skin is so soft,' he said, looking at her mouth. 'And I have dreamed of your mouth.'

She lifted her head and groaned. 'It's not even dark!'

Emilio threw back his head and laughed. The deep, attractive sound lowered the sexual temperature but the respite was brief. A moment later he was looking at her, his teeth bared in a white, wolfish grin, and the expression of predatory intent written into every line of his lean face as he looked down at her sent the sexual temperature zooming off the chart!

'Are you a lights-out girl?'

She was a good-book-and-a-mug-of-cocoa girl, but even had she felt inclined to confess this Megan doubted he would have believed her.

'While I agree darkness has an allure,' he continued in the same deep, seductive, throaty purr that made the downy hair on her neck and arms rise and the skin they covered tingle. 'It breaks down restraints and frees up the imagination.'

Megan, whose imagination had broken free of all her own restraints, her eyes sealed to his, began to pant softly. She couldn't seem to draw enough air into her tight, aching chest.

'I find visual stimulus very—'

With a cry she pulled her hands out from between their bodies and clamped them over her ears, closing her eyes and yelling, 'We weren't talking about your sexual predilections!'

A static silence followed her outburst. Megan stood there with her eyes tight shut, knowing she had pretty much blown her I've-been-here-done-this-got-the-T-shirt card!

'No, we were talking about yours.'

At the quiet but firm correction her eyes flickered open. She angled a wary look at his face and immediately felt her defences crumble as she read tenderness mingled in with the driven hunger in his lean face.

'I would like to know what pleases you.'

The answer did not require much thought and Megan felt her knees give as the truth emerged uncensored from her lips. 'You!'

Heat flared hot in Emilio's eyes in response to her whispered admission.

Megan could not understand a word of the flood of liquid, passionate Spanish that flowed from his lips, but she listened raptly, observing with a mixture of anticipation and apprehension the smile of gloating male satisfaction that curved his sensually sculpted lips.

'I don't know what you just said, but—'

He cut her off, which was possibly just as well because Megan hadn't the faintest idea what she wanted to say. What sort of *but* was appropriate after you'd just told a man that he virtually embodied your sexual fantasies? There was actually no virtual about it—he did!

'I said I intend to please you,' he promised thickly.

Megan's heart lurched wildly further south; the liquid heat between her thighs throbbed. She never doubted for a moment that he could fulfil his promise and she couldn't wait—it was what she wanted.

It was what she'd always wanted.

You can't have what you want. You can just have a tiny piece of it. Will that be enough?

Megan lifted her chin and silenced the whisper of doubt in her head. You had to take a risk. Life was short and when it threw the possibility of something precious your way it would be churlish, not to mention stupid, not to grab it with both hands!

The alternative was always wondering what if? Megan didn't want what ifs. She wanted Emilio. She wanted Emilio heavy on top of her; she wanted him inside her.

For the first time she allowed herself to look at him without trying to disguise what she was feeling. The sensation was simultaneously liberating and scary, but since when was anything that involved Emilio uncomplicated?

'I want you so badly, Emilio, I can't stand up.'

Megan heard the sharp intake of his breath and sighed as his long fingers slid into her silky hair. Her head fell back, the expression in her golden eyes hazed by a sheen of lust as he slid a supporting second hand into her hair and angled her face up to him.

'You are so beautiful—that face, that body.'

Megan saw the raw hunger in his eyes and tasted for the first time some of the female power he had spoken of—it felt pretty good. She wanted to tell him it was the first time she'd felt this way, that he was the first man who—

Her eyes widened. God, she had to warn him that she hadn't done this before it went any further, even at the risk of her confession ruining the mood. The possibility of that happening made her hold back, but only for a moment. If he had a problem with her inexperience it was better to know now, not later down the line.

Rejection later on really would be crushing.

'Do you remember that night in the car?'

Emilio swore softly under his breath at the reintroduction of the subject.

Obviously he remembers, stupid, she told herself. He thinks it's the event that triggered your moral downfall.

'Well, I know that it looked—'

'I remember that that night I came this close…' he interrupted, bringing his face within a whisper of hers.

Megan's eyelids drooped. She could feel the waft of his warm breath on her skin, on her mouth. The thought of confession slipped from her head as lust and longing shuddered through her body. She stared transfixed at the fine lines around his eyes, the gold tips at the end of his otherwise ebony eyelashes. Her heart ached. He was the most breathtaking, perfect thing on the planet and he wanted her.

'This close?' she parroted, fighting her way through the sensual fog in her head.

'To throttling the bastard,' he explained matter-of-factly.

Not following this instinct had taken a large chunk of will power, but the effort had faded into insignificance beside the will power he had needed to tap into to stop himself taking Megan in his arms to comfort her.

The sight of her standing there, white-faced and shaking, looking so vulnerable and fragile, had awoken every protective instinct he had and some new ones. While she had struggled not to cry he had struggled to keep his distance.

Emilio hadn't allowed himself to even touch her.

He couldn't. If he had he knew it wouldn't have stopped at comforting.

He had been tempted. *Dios*, but he had been so tempted standing there, fighting against his baser instincts, especially given the status of his relationship with his then wife playing in a loop through his head.

Little snippets of the beginning of the end of his marriage slid into his head now.

'I understand,' Rosanna said when she discovered he had removed his things from the room they shared.

'And are relieved?' he asked, genuinely curious, and taking no satisfaction from her obvious distress.

Emilio felt a lot of responsibility for what had happened. His mindset when he had entered into the marriage had not differed from how he would enter into any other contract.

With the benefit of hindsight he could see that this had been a mistake—this wasn't any contract.

Mistake number two had been not factoring in the

emotional factor, not allowing for the possibility that, despite what she had said, Rosanna needed more than he had been prepared or able to offer.

What had happened had been inevitable.

The suggestion made his errant wife look uncomfortable. 'I wasn't dissatisfied with what we had. That isn't why I slept with—'

Emilio took pity on her. 'It's all right, I don't want a score out of ten, Rosanna, and I don't want to know his name.'

'I know you don't. If you'd loved me you would have.'

'I never—'

'I know you didn't,' she cut in quickly. '*He* didn't love me either, but he said that he did, and I needed to hear that even if it was a lie,' she admitted sadly. 'Don't look like that, Emilio. Don't be sorry for me. I'm not asking you to sleep with me. I don't expect it, and I do realise that you will need—when you do I won't make a fuss.'

'So you are giving me permission to have sex with other women?'

'It's a sensible solution.'

Cold-blooded and clinical were the words that slid unexpectedly into Emilio's mind; they were two things that he had been accused of in the past. And mostly those accusations had been justified, so why now did settling for a dispassionate solution make him feel discontent?

Why did he think it was settling? *Settling* implied there was a better option. He knew there wasn't—marriage was by definition flawed, at best a compromise.

'More sensible than a divorce?'

She looked at him, white with anxiety under the perfect make-up he had never seen her without. 'But you agreed we could make this work.'

'I agreed that a divorce would be messy. I agreed that we

make better friends than lovers. I agreed that domesticity is not something I am suited to.'

'You haven't met anyone?' she began tentatively. 'Someone special?'

The idea amused him. 'I have met no one I wish to have sex with and, even if I had, I have no desire to leap into another marriage,' he promised, believing it.

They left it like that.

When six months passed and he had not taken up the offer of guilt-free cheating, he did pause to consider the situation. Six months was a long time and he was a man with a healthy sex drive. He recognised channelling his energies, no matter how successfully, into work was not a long-term solution to the problem.

Did his reluctance to even acknowledge a problem existed stem from the fact he still thought of sex outside marriage as *cheating*?

It was not a distaste of cheating that held him in check when he looked at Megan that night and burnt with a primal need to make her his.

It was the knowledge that following through with his instincts, taking advantage of her at a moment like this would make him no better than the man he had just sent packing.

The idea filled him with repugnance; for the first time in his life he wanted more than sex. He did not want some sordid hole-in-the-corner affair; he did not want their relationship to be tarnished with his past mistakes. He knew he had to be patient.

Despite his reputation for infallibility, Emilio had made bad decisions in the past. While he did not advertise that, neither did he agonise over it; he shrugged and moved on.

But the decision he made that night to be patient had not

been one he had been able to shrug away. It had tortured Emilio for two years.

He never made the same mistake twice.

Emilio was going to make Megan Armstrong his. He was going to make her forget every man she had ever known. Determination hardened to steel inside him. The need to claim her had not lessened with time, but deepened—she was going to be his.

He ran a finger down her smooth cheek, smiling as he felt her shudder. He breathed in the fragrance of her hair and allowed the scent of apples to flood his senses.

'I did not warm to the man,' he explained.

Megan, deep in the sensual thrall, responded to the wry admission with a vague, 'Who?' The warmth of his breath on her ear lobe was sending shivers of sensation all the way down to her curling toes.

He brought his face close to hers until their noses were almost touching. 'The clown you were fighting off in the car.'

'I *was* fighting him off,' she said, thinking, Kiss me, please kiss me. Every second he didn't was sheer torture.

'I know.' He lifted his head fractionally and hooked a thumb under her chin, tilting her head from side to side as he studied the soft curves of her face with an expression of ferocious fascination. 'I should have throttled him,' he mused thickly. 'I *really* wanted to, but not as much as I wanted to do this.'

Without warning he grabbed her bottom, his big hands curling over the feminine curves as he hauled her upwards and hard against his body, sealing them from waist to thigh.

Megan's eyes flew wide, the breath leaving her body in

a gusty sigh as she registered the bold imprint of his rock-hard erection as it ground into the softness of her belly.

'Oh, God!' she groaned as a rush of liquid heat exploded inside her. 'You wanted… That night… But you were married.'

His mouth twisted into a smile that left his dark eyes cold. 'Do you think that a piece of paper stops a man wanting another woman? You of all people should know that isn't so, Megan.'

She flinched at the reference. 'So you're saying if it did I wouldn't exist,' she said quietly, trying not to be shocked by his admission. Maybe some men shouldn't get married. Especially highly sexed ones like Emilio.

He kissed her then, hard and possessively, the bruising pressure of his lips driving the breath from her lungs, his tongue probing deep into her mouth. Megan's arms slid around his middle as she clung, kissing him back wildly, without finesse, just with a hunger that equalled his.

When he finally lifted his mouth from hers it took several seconds for her head to clear, for a tiny sliver of sanity to filter back.

'You're going to do that again, aren't you?' Not that much sanity.

He smiled, his liquid, dark, incredible eyes fastened on to her face absorbing every detail as he ran his fingers down her throat. 'That's up to you.'

His reply frustrated her. 'Do I have to beg?'

No wonder he looked so smugly confident; he had to have had women begging him all his life.

God knew Megan didn't want to be another notch on his bedpost, but if she had to beg she would. Where Emilio was concerned it seemed she had no pride.

'You have to tell me you want me as much as I want you.'

She began to turn her head, her lips trembling. 'Because you don't know.'

The bitterness in her voice brought a frown to his face. 'Because I need to hear you say it.'

She couldn't bear it. Every cell in her body craved his touch. 'I want you, Emilio.'

His nostrils flared as he moved in to bite her lower lip, breathing in her warm womanly smell as he nipped his way towards the corner of her mouth. 'But if you prefer to go sightseeing…' he teased, running his tongue along the sensitive skin of her inner lip. Her moan of pained protest drew a fierce grin from Emilio. 'Though I should point out that my bedroom is much closer…'

If they got that far it would be a miracle. He was clinging to what control he had with his fingernails. To have her shaking with lust for him was incredible and her wild response had blown him away. All he could think about was burying himself in her.

Megan's head fell back to look into his lean face. Her eyes were half closed, her cheeks flushed. 'Bed, please.'

A low growl vibrated in Emilio's throat as his hold tightened, his arms like steel bands around her ribcage as he bit and nuzzled his way up the exposed curve of her white neck.

Megan went limp in his arms, her eyelashes fluttering like butterfly wings against her flushed cheeks, her toes brushing the ground as Emilio walked blindly across the room to the bedroom door, his lips moving up the curve of her throat.

He reached the door and her lips at the same moment. Keeping his dark eyes trained on her face, his mouth a tantalising whisper from her own, Emilio hefted her higher into his arms as though she weighed nothing, an arm scooping her bottom as he swung her upwards. She shivered, some buried primal instinct in her responding to the raw power revealed in his casual action.

CHAPTER ELEVEN

'KISS me, Megan!' Emilio rasped, and kicked open the door, the instruction and action blending seamlessly into one.

The door hit the wall behind with a loud crash, the vibration of the impact rippling around the apartment as Megan, her eyes glowing, grabbed his face between her hands and pressed her warm lips to his.

Her enthusiasm drew a growl of approval from his throat, then as she slid her tongue experimentally into his mouth, tentatively and then with more confidence, she felt a shudder run through his lean body.

She stopped kissing him long enough to moan, 'God, you taste so good.'

Emilio's eyes darkened dramatically. *'Madre de Dios!'*

'Is something wrong?' she asked anxiously. He looked like someone in pain.

'Wrong?' he echoed. He looked at her, his brilliant eyes fierce but tender, the muscles in his brown throat visibly working as he swallowed, struggling to control the primal hunger pounding through his body. 'No, things are very right. You wish to taste me, you shall,' he told her thickly. 'But not until I have sampled every inch of your delicious body.'

The throaty promise planted a mental image in Megan's head that made her skin prickle.

His long-legged stride brought them to the bed in seconds. Megan's eyes were closed and her arms still fastened around his neck as he lowered her onto the bed.

As she sank into the mattress Megan opened her eyes.

Emilio curved over her, motionless; his breath came harder as he looked down at her. 'You're beautiful,' Emilio slurred, his voice thick with desire. 'I've never in my life needed anything as much as I need you.'

The husky confession sent a thrill through Megan's tense, aching body. She waited, her heart beating frantically in anticipation as she stared into his glowing midnight-dark eyes.

She wanted his touch, she ached for his kisses, she wanted him with a fierce urgency that scared her. For a second she wanted to retreat from it, push him away, but she made herself accept it, embrace it.

In that moment her last doubts vanished in a blaze of certainty.

This was what she wanted. The *rightness* of it made no sense, but that didn't matter. Unable to communicate the ache of inarticulate yearning that brought the threat of tears to her eyes, Megan raised her arms, stretching her finger towards him in a silent plea.

The gesture cut through Emilio's last shred of control. A growl locked in his throat, his face set in a strained mask of primal need. He caught her hands, raised them to his lips and pressed his lips to each palm in turn before he sat down on the edge of the bed.

Retaining her hands in his, he placed them against his chest.

Megan could feel the heat of his body through his shirt. With a soft cry she pulled herself into a sitting position and began to fumble with the buttons on his shirt with frenzied urgency. Her hands were shaking so much that the simple task was beyond her.

'Let me.'

A hand in the middle of her chest sent Megan back against the pillows.

Megan watched through half-closed eyes, her throat dry and aching as he slipped the buttons of his shirt, his actions tantalisingly slow.

The fabric parted to reveal his taut muscled torso, his broad, well-developed chest and flat, muscle-ridged belly. His skin gleamed like beaten copper.

Megan gasped. 'Oh, God!' and ran her tongue across the surface of her dry lips.

There was predatory confidence in his smile as he fought his way out of his shirt and flung it across the room.

Megan couldn't take her eyes off him. His skin glowed and he didn't carry an ounce of surplus flesh on his sleek, muscular body.

He almost casually pinioned her hands either side of her head before settling his long, lean length down beside her. There was nothing casual about the searing heat of his stare as ran his tongue up the exposed curve of her neck.

'You taste good.'

He lowered his head towards her, but at the last second stopped just short of her mouth and looked deep into her eyes, part of him wanting to prolong the moment he had waited for.

'Please kiss me, Emilio.'

The husky plea snapped the last thread of his shredded control. A deep groan emerged from his lips as he sealed his mouth to hers, pressing her limp body deep into the mattress with the force of his kiss.

Megan gave a soft moan of yearning as her lips parted

under the hungry, demanding pressure. The sound was lost
in his mouth as his tongue stabbed deep, the erotic incur-
sions drawing a series of mewling sounds of pleasure from
her throat.

'This is crazy.'

He trailed a series of moist, open-mouthed kisses down
her throat. 'You want me and I want you. Is that crazy?'

'Yes, it is, but I think I like crazy.'

He levered himself up a little to allow himself easier
access to the buttons on her blouse. He started at the bottom
and worked his way upwards, holding her eyes, watching
her gasp as each one gave way.

Megan squeezed her eyes closed and held her breath
as he peeled the fabric aside. At the sound of his rasping
intake of breath, her eyes shot open.

He was staring transfixed at her body; desire burned in
his eyes like twin flames. '*Por Dios*, but you are lovely,'
he breathed, his expression almost reverent as his glance
licked down her pale body.

She glowed. Her skin was as pale as alabaster, not cold,
but warm. Megan was warm. Emilio wanted to bury himself in her warmth, feel it close tight around him.

Megan shivered, the earthy appreciation in his deep
voice sending an erotic thrill through her body. She shivered again and bit her lip, oblivious to the pain as he traced
a line with his finger down the middle of her stomach before
laying his big hand across the curve of her stomach.

Then, holding her eyes, he unclipped the front catch on
her bra.

His eyes left her then, and she heard the breath leave his
lungs in a long, sibilant hiss. His eyes glittered with passion
as he curved his shaking hand around one soft, pink-tipped
mound, drawing an earthy moan from her throat as he
rubbed his thumb across the engorged peak before taking

it into his mouth. All the time his fingers were stroking her delicate skin with erotic skill that made her burn up inside with the nameless need that gripped her.

She writhed in a sweet torment, her response to his skilful caresses uncoordinated, the words that slipped from her lips unintelligible in the hot haze of passion.

One hand stayed curved possessively around her breast as he lifted his head and looked deep into her passion-glazed tawny eyes before he bent his head, his tongue dipping inside the parted pink sweetness between her lips, drawing a series of weak cries of pleasure from Megan.

He slid a hand around her back, drawing her up off the bed while he freed the blouse and bra from her shaking body. One arm wrapped around her narrow ribcage, the other pressed behind her head, he lay down, drawing her down beside him.

The first skin-to-skin contact was shocking, then, after the shock faded, addictive. Megan's mind emptied, she stopped thinking, acting on the dormant instincts that surfaced as she pressed her breasts against the hard barrier of his hair-roughened chest.

Emilio continued to kiss her, one deep drowning kiss blending into the next.

When he eventually drew back the naked desire shining in his dark eyes sent a fresh pulse of desire slamming through her body.

'Hold that thought,' he said thickly as he rolled on his back. Megan's instinctive protest stilled as she watched him unfasten his belt, lifting his narrow hips off the bed to slide them down his thighs, then kick them away.

His boxers received the same treatment.

Megan felt the hot colour score her cheeks; he was aroused and he was magnificent! Heat pulsed, spreading from her core through her body, and the dragging, heavy sensation low in her pelvis became a physical pain. She couldn't take her eyes off him.

Emilio saw her staring and didn't seem to mind. In fact on physical evidence her unconcealed awe appeared to arouse him further—something she would have imagined was impossible!

He swung his legs around the side of the bed, his movements as graceful and sinuous as a big cat, each action emphasising the controlled strength and power of his body. She wondered at his complete lack of self-consciousness, her covetous gaze following his progress around to her side of the bed.

By the time he stood over her she was so aroused by the erotic image he presented that breathing was a struggle. Each laboured inhalation she drew made her full breasts quiver.

Without a word he bent down, one knee braced on the bed, and slipped a hand under the waistband of her skirt. The contact of his fingers on her burning skin sent a shiver along her sensitised nerve endings.

She closed her eyes as he slid her skirt down her thighs, then closed them tighter still as he removed her tiny briefs.

'Look at me, Megan.'

Megan prised her heavy lids open and gazed up at him, mute with helpless longing.

Raw need burning in his eyes, Emilio took her fingers and curled them around his erection. 'This is how much I want you,' he slurred.

It was, Megan thought, quite a lot!

She stroked him, her fingers tightened around his throbbing length. Emilio closed his eyes and groaned before gritting his teeth and removing her clever fingers forcibly before he ran his own fingers along the silky curve of her inner thigh, smiling with primitive satisfaction to hear her gasp, then moan as he parted her legs, opening her to him.

He kneeled over her. She was the most beautiful thing he had ever seen, ravishing. The need inside him was pounding in his head, wiping every thought but the need to possess her from his mind.

His entire being was focused on one thing—making her his, binding her to him.

As he kneeled between her legs he was unable to resist the lure of her quivering swollen lips. He kissed her lips hard, then the curve of her belly, before his smoky dark eyes meshed with her slumberous golden gaze.

He reached between her legs, her body arched in response to the intimate touch, the slick heat he discovered there, the knowledge that she was ready for him, and then finally her husky plea of, 'Please, Emilio,' broke his control.

His face contorted in a fierce mask of driving need, he settled between her legs, his body curved over her.

Megan felt the push against her silken barrier and tensed at the exact moment he slid into her. The cry of shock and pain was wrenched from her throat.

Above her he froze. He had felt the resistance at the last moment and understood what it meant, but it had been too late to pull back.

'Relax,' he soothed, kissing her neck.

'I'm… You're…' A long sigh left her throat as her tense muscle unclenched and began to expand to accommodate him. The sensation was incredible and as he began to move very slowly the fibres inside her responded to the friction, sending hot fingers of sensation rippling through her entire body.

'Oh, yes!' she sighed, grabbing his shoulder for support as she relaxed into the rhythm as he sank deeper into her.

Sweat slicked Emilio's body as he fought with every fibre of his being to control his thrusts, though in that final moment when he felt the deep contractions of her climax build he let go and slammed into her, feeling his explosive release and a moment later the guilt.

CHAPTER TWELVE

FINALLY Emilio rolled off her. Megan missed the weight of him pressing her into the mattress. Without the heat of his body the air-conditioned air felt cool on her hot, sweat-slick skin.

Megan, her breathing still all over the place, turned her head on the pillow. Emilio lay beside her on his back, one arm curved above his head. His eyes were closed and he was breathing deeply; his chest rose and fell in sync with each shallow breath. Megan rested her cheek in the crook of her arm, her expression rapt as she followed the play of muscles sliding below the golden glistening surface.

Everything about him fascinated her.

She reached out a hand to touch his skin and drew back. So far he hadn't said a word. Was that normal? Should she be bothered by his silence?

How crazy was this? Minutes earlier they had been intimate in a way that should have shocked her but hadn't; now she was scared of touching him in case it was the wrong thing.

Megan chewed her lower lip fretfully as the doubts crowded in. Had he fallen asleep?

Perhaps he would expect to find her dressed or even gone when he woke up? The instincts that had kicked in earlier had definitely switched off.

It was ironic—when she might have expected to feel some uncertainty there had been none, except for that brief moment when she was sure that they were simply not compatible in a purely dimensional sense—she had been very pleased to be proved wrong.

Beautifully wrong!

She might no longer be a virtuous virgin, but she still had no clue how a person was meant to behave post-lovemaking.

She glanced around the unfamiliar bedroom with the vast bed and modern art on the walls almost guiltily, as though she were a voyeur intruding on a scene in someone else's life.

But this wasn't happening to someone else, it was happening to her. Had happened.

No wonder it seemed surreal. *I spent the morning in bed with Emilio Rios*—now how weird did that sound? Actually, not so weird at all. A person, it seemed, could adapt awfully quickly to some things.

But she couldn't allow herself to lose sight of the fact that for Emilio this was just sex. While in one sense his pragmatic approach to his physical needs and appetites shocked Megan, in another way she did kind of admire his painful honesty.

It would never be possible for her to match his honesty, she thought, refusing to acknowledge the lonely ache in her heart—time enough for that later. To him she was a one-night or any rate one-morning stand, so wanting more was a stupid waste of time.

She had always wanted more from him. God, it really did stink when your first crush turned out to be your last!

She had always been his for the taking; he just hadn't felt the urge to reach before today. Megan blinked away the hot tears burning behind her eyes and gave a fierce frown

as she told herself that for once in her life she would not
think about tomorrow.

Her eyes made a covetous sweep of his body. A natural
athlete's body, long and lean, it was a sculpted, breathing
miracle of taut muscles, hard bone and glistening, satiny
bronzed skin. A tiny sigh of appreciation left her lips; he
really was beautiful!

And he had done beautiful things to her.

*And tomorrow he would be doing them to someone
else.*

The pucker between her arched brows smoothed out
as she firmly pushed away the thought. She swallowed,
refusing to acknowledge the ache in her throat—why spoil
a perfect moment?

She rolled onto her side, watching the rise and fall of
his chest as Emilio sucked air deep into his lungs through
flared nostrils. There was not the slightest suggestion of
softness in any part of his lean, hard body. She exhaled a
shaky sigh and thought, This *is* perfect.

He was perfect.

As she watched him, need unfurled from the tight knot
of nameless emotions locked in her chest. She had imagined
she was in love with him, but the man she had fallen for
had never really existed. She had been infatuated with a
fantasy.

She had seen the real Emilio Rios the night he had
ripped her character to shreds, not a kind man, but dangerous and capable, as she knew to her cost, of being cruel.

She tried to work out the attraction. She knew it wasn't
just his amazing face or athlete's body. Emilio projected
a raw power, an intensity that drew her like a moth to a
flame.

Scratch the surface of polished sophistication he was
famed for and there was something primitive, a danger that

should logically have made her run. Instead Megan found his earthy magnetism impossible to resist.

Throat thick with emotion that shone in her amber eyes, she responded to the compelling need to touch him. She reached out, tangling her fingers in the light fuzz of hair on his chest before trailing her fingers slowly in the direction of his flat, muscle-ridged belly. She had never imagined feeling this greedy fascination with a man's body, but she was utterly enthralled by everything, from the texture of his skin to the faint quiver of muscles just under the satiny surface she stroked.

The dark fan of his ebony lashes lifted slowly from the sharp angle of his cheekbones.

Megan held her breath.

Emilio turned his head.

Their eyes connected, liquid brown on topaz.

She could not read the expression in his dark eyes but she could feel the waves of strong emotion rolling off him, not something she had anticipated.

Neither had she anticipated the wave of paralysing shyness, not after the intimacies they had just shared and the total lack of inhibition she had displayed. She lay there aware of every imperfection, feeling horribly exposed and vulnerable, wishing with every ounce of her being that she could recapture the liberating pleasure in her own body she had experienced while they had been making love.

Emilio's stare had not wavered from her face. The intensity of his unblinking regard was starting to be unsettling, but suddenly overwhelmingly conscious of her nakedness Megan reached down for a sheet to cover herself.

The next seconds were a blur. One moment she was clumsily attempting to grab the sheet, the next her hands were pinioned above her head.

'What are you doing?'

'I should get dressed.' It was pretty hard to hit a casual note, but Megan thought she did quite well given the circumstances. 'I'm sure you have things to do, a busy schedule, and I should touch base with D—'

'You should stop babbling.'

'I'm not babbling,' she protested.

His broad shoulders lifted fractionally. 'All right, talking nonsense.' His dark eyes dropped from her face, sliding slowly down her body.

The insolent, sexually overt scrutiny made her stomach muscles twist in excitement.

'I do have things to do.' His eyes glittered as he bared his white teeth in a fierce smile. 'All of them include you, and clothes are not involved. Your body pleases me. I find it utterly and totally exquisite. You will not hide it from me. You should be proud of it and enjoy it as much as I intend to.'

The explosive quality in his fierce stare made her shiver, then cry out without warning he pressed his face against her breasts, the stubble on his chin abrading the smooth, sensitive skin, but not in a bad way.

He thinks I'm beautiful.

Her breath came in a series of shallow gasps as, eyes half closed, she watched through heavy eyelids his dark head against her body, her back arching as his tongue began to whip slowly across the peaks of her breasts, still painfully sensitised from their recent lovemaking.

When he loosed her hands to cup one quivering peak she tangled her fingers in his dark hair, pushing through the ebony strands still damp from their recent exertions to cradle his skull and hold him against her.

They stayed in his hair when he lifted his head and grinned down at her.

'Also there is no point trying to hide from me in a bed this small.'

The bed was vast but she let it pass. 'I wasn't trying to hide,' she protested.

He arched an ironic brow, making her eyes slide guiltily from his.

'I was cold.'

'Cold?' Emilio laid his hand possessively on the soft feminine curve of her stomach. Megan started and trembled at his touch, shifting restlessly under his hand, but not wanting it to go away.

'You do not feel cold to me.' He leaned across her, sealing his mouth to hers as he kissed her, and he ran his hands down the silky skin of her thighs, wresting a whimper from her throat.

'Not cold at all.'

Eyes closed, her head fell to one side as he began to nuzzle her neck.

Emilio's head lifted, but his eyes remained riveted on her raspberry-pink thrusting nipples, wet and gleaming from his recent ministrations, dark against the milk-pale skin of her perfect breasts. With the utmost reluctance he clenched his jaw and tore his gaze free of temptation.

'We have things to talk about,' Megan heard him say with some unease.

She opened her eyes. 'I thought you were a man of action, not words.' Would the challenge successfully divert him?

It didn't. Emilio saw through her tactics. 'Nice try,' he admired sardonically. 'And I am tempted,' he admitted with a smile that made her heart flip. The smile was absent as he added in a voice stripped of the sexy smokiness, 'But we will talk. Your economy with words and my actions could have hurt you.'

He stopped and moved a hand across his face. She was shocked when his hand fell away to see his face contorted in a grimace of self-loathing.

'*Did* hurt you,' he added sombrely.

Megan was shaken by the dark anguish she saw reflected in the shadows of his incredible eyes. 'No…' she protested. 'No, you didn't.' The memory of the moment of pain had already faded, supplanted by the incredible pleasure that had followed.

The muscles in Emilio's brown throat stood out corded with tension as he dragged a hand jerkily across the surface of his dark hair, making it stand up spikily in front.

It was, she decided, a good look on him, but then any look was good on Emilio. God, but I am so besotted.

'Do not lie to me, Megan,' he rasped throatily as he caught her jaw between his long fingers and angled her face to him.

Megan struggled to judge his mood; his enigmatic expression gave nothing away. 'I'm not—'

'You have never been with a man before.' The shock still fresh in his mind, Emilio struggled to frame the words. 'It was your first time.'

If he pursued the theme too far Megan knew there was a real danger of her revealing more than was sensible.

The last thing she wanted was Emilio knowing that she had only been a virgin, not because she was virtuous or even that she had major hang-ups about sex, but because… God, how could she admit, without sounding incredibly old-fashioned, that she'd made a choice early on not to have sex outside marriage?

Megan had simply never been able to imagine being intimate with a man she didn't have a strong emotional connection with.

The man she slept with would be the man she fell in love

with, and as the only man she'd ever fallen for had been married she had accepted it might never happen and she was fine with that, or so she had told herself. There was more to life than sex and there were few things worse in life, it seemed to her, than sex with the wrong man.

There had been a lot of wrong men for her mother, a parade of 'uncles' whom Megan could recall appearing and disappearing at intervals. The eternal optimist, Clare Smith had always embarked on a new relationship believing it was *the* one, only to end up crushed and heartbroken when things fell apart.

As she got older and recognised the destructive pattern Megan, not sharing her mother's optimism, had begun to dread seeing a new man appear. Some of the youthful anger she felt had been aimed at her mother; she wished very much now she had been more understanding.

'Why do you need a man?' she had yelled. 'Why can't I be enough?'

The stricken look on her mother's face had stayed with her and she had never had an opportunity to retract it. Her mother had slipped off a crowded pavement at rush hour and under the wheels of a passing bus.

A hissing expletive left Emilio's lips as, face dark with wrath, he stared at her, the muscle in his lean cheek spasmodically clenching and unclenching.

He looked ready to implode.

Megan struggled to respond to the blunt statement of her virginal status without blushing and failed. 'Guilty as charged,' she joked in an attempt to play the subject down.

Megan bit her lip. So much for lightening the mood!

'You think this a joke?' he grated. 'Your first time should be *special*.'

Megan stared and thought, And he thinks it wasn't?

'I may not have used the word,' she told him in a voice that shook with the emotions she was struggling to suppress, 'but if you're talking *special* as in unique and outstandingly brilliant, I do seem to recall saying something along those lines, quite loudly actually.'

'You're blushing, all over.' The discovery appeared to distract and amuse him, though a moment later he was looking darkly sombre once more as he picked up a theme that Megan found acutely uncomfortable.

'Your first time only happens the once, and...and I...' His face contorted with a grimace of self-disgust, he broke off and dragged a hand down his jaw. Hearing the sound in his head, he felt as if he'd never be able to forget her sharp cry. His voice dropped as he accused, 'You wept.'

Silently, and he had held her shaking body and felt like a total animal.

Megan laid a tentative hand on his shoulder; his muscles felt rock-hard and rigid. 'It wasn't because you hurt me,' she protested, stunned by his reading of the situation.

'If I had known—' His jaw clenched; the knowledge that he had hurt her felt like a blade sliding between his ribs. 'But how could you be... *Why?*'

Megan groaned and scanned his face. 'You're not going to let this go, are you?'

He looked at her as though she had just announced she was actually a Martian. *'Let it go!'* He'd waited two years for that moment and when it had happened he had blown it! When he thought of the way he had... *'Por Dios!* I think you owe me an explanation,' he announced grimly.

Her eyes slid guiltily from his. *I'm yours and I love you. I actually pretty much always have*, was a fairly accurate summing-up of the situation, but she doubted it would go down too well.

'Why the hell didn't you tell me that you—?'

Her voice tight with humiliation, Megan cut across his incensed demand. 'You didn't seem all that interested in conversation at the time.'

The line of colour across the angle of Emilio's cheekbones deepened as their glances clashed. Even now the air between them hummed with a sexual tension that was almost tangible. Despite the intensity of their lovemaking it had not even taken the edge off his hunger for her.

He did not need reminding that his actions had been ruled by his own selfish carnal desire, a carnal desire that after two years of denial had been stripped to its primitive and most basic form.

It had been a point of pride with Emilio that he had never been a victim of his hormones. He had certainly never lost control in bed before, and now the one time he should have shown restraint with a woman, when he should have been gentle, he had snapped. His relentless, ravenous need for her had made him utterly blind to her inexperience until that last moment.

There must have been clues? How had he missed them? Missed the opportunity to make her initiation special.

'And you were not acting like a virgin,' corrosive shame made him retort defensively.

'Know a lot about virgins, do you?'

His eyes narrowed as his eyes drifted to her tender lips still swollen from his kisses. 'Nothing, as it happens,' he said, thinking it seemed he also knew even less about women, or this one at least.

'You're making a big thing of nothing. Being a virgin isn't like having a contagious disease. It's not obligatory to go into isolation.' Her mouth settled into a mutinous line of defiance as she tried to hide her hurt. 'I'm sorry you feel cheated and short-changed but I'm not about to say sorry.'

His brows lifted. 'What are you talking about now? *Cheated…?*' he asked irritably. 'You are not making sense.'

Face scrunched in an effort to hold back the tears that threatened to spill over, she lifted her chin and blinked hard.

'Well, so sorry,' she drawled, 'if I've lost my edge of clinical objectivity, but I've never been in this situation before.'

'And you think I have?'

'Yes, I get it, you don't need to spell it out.' She had been slow but the penny had finally dropped. She knew why he was acting this way. 'You thought you were getting someone who knew what she was doing in the bedroom and instead—' she broke off to give a loud sniff and passed a hand across her suspiciously bright eyes as she gulped '—instead you got me.'

She heard the unattractive, self-pitying whine in her voice and shook her head, mumbling, 'Even you could not have got it perfect your first time.'

He probably had. Megan closed her eyes, hating the woman he had got it right with.

Torn between frustration and tenderness, Emilio levered himself into a sitting position with the fluid grace that typified all his actions.

'Have I got this right?' he asked, placing one hand beside her head as he looked down at her. 'You think I feel *short-changed*? *Short-changed?*' he repeated, shaking his head as he added something, not appearing to realise he had slipped into his native tongue, and laughed. 'The way your mind works, *querida*, is a constant source of amazement to me. Listen, you may not value what you gave me highly, but I do.'

CHAPTER THIRTEEN

MEGAN'S eyes slid slowly up from the expanse of golden chest she was staring at. 'You value?'

She parroted the words like someone speaking a foreign language.

Emilio nodded and framed her face between his long brown fingers, smoothing the strands of hair spread around her face from her brow. 'I am your first.' The sheer impossibility of it still shook him. 'Do you know how that makes me feel?'

Her eyes darted from side to side, refusing to meet his. 'Annoyed?'

'Privileged.'

She froze at the throaty rebuttal, her eyes heavy, lids half closing as he touched her cheek. The tremor she felt in his fingers as they brushed slowly across the downy curve shocked her.

Her lips, soft and warm and so incredibly sweet, trembled under his as he kissed her softly.

'And in shock,' he admitted, pulling back. 'I still don't understand how it is possible.'

Arm curved above her head, she watched as he propped his broad shoulders against the carved headboard. Taking a deep breath, she pushed the tangled strands off her hot face with one hand and, anchoring the sheet over her breasts with the other, pulled herself up into a kneeling position.

'Because you thought I slept my way through college?'

The suggestion drew a dark frown from Emilio. 'No, because you've been living with a man for two years.' And though he had buried it deep, the knowledge had driven him out of his mind. He took a deep breath, let the anger pass through him and released it; despite a lot of practice he had never quite perfected the technique.

'A man!' Megan sank deeper into confusion.

'All right, live-in lover, boyfriend, whatever he was to you.'

Megan sat back on her heels, lifting a hand to balance herself as the mattress shifted. She was totally at sea. Live-in lover? She had barely had a date!

'What are you talking about? I haven't been living with a man!' She stopped, her eyes widening in comprehension, before sliding back down in the bed with a laugh and a billowing of silken sheets. 'You're talking about Josh?' She chuckled.

He arched a brow, his focus drifting as his eyes were drawn to the outline of her body against the silk. She gave a sinuous wriggle. All he had to do was reach out and lift the sheet… He swallowed as he struggled to banish the image of her smooth, naked body from his head.

The effort made sweat break out along his upper lip.

'There were others?' He immediately recognised the irrationality, given the topic under discussion, of his jealous question. More? There hadn't been any!

'What is this about?'

Emilio looked down at her lying there, looking like a wild-haired wanton angel, and felt a pulse of desire throb through his body. 'That's what I'm trying to find out. This *Josh*, he—'

Megan's brows twitched into a perplexed line. Her fingers restlessly tugged at the sheet. 'What is this thing you have about Josh? You sound as if you don't like him.'

'I have no thing about *Josh*. I'm sure he was perfect, but…'

'Pretty much,' she admitted. It was a view shared by all her female friends. They had all bemoaned the fact that the perfect men were always gay.

The smiling insertion drew a dark frown from Emilio. 'You lived with the man!'

His accusing manner and bewildering interest in the subject of her ex-flatmate was beginning to make Megan feel angry. 'It's hardly a crime to share a flat with someone and I'm not on trial,' she added, growing more bewildered by the second—his condemnatory attitude. 'What has living with Josh got to do with anything?'

'You have been living with the man for two years. What am I to think you spend your time doing? Playing Scrabble? *Por Dios!*' His upper lip curled in a derisive sneer as he shook his dark head slowly from side to side. It was inexplicable to him that any man could live under the same roof as Megan for two hours and not make love to her—this man had spent two years!

She stopped, her startled stare flying to his face as the penny finally dropped. 'Josh—my boyfriend!'

'What was he waiting for—your wedding night?' Emilio growled.

The question touched a nerve with Megan. 'And would that be so weird?' she asked him sharply.

Emilio stared at her. 'In one word—yes.'

'Well, call me weird but actually that was my plan up until an hour or so ago.'

It turned out it was easy to have lofty principles when there was no temptation. Not that she regretted her change of heart for a millisecond.

He swore under his breath.

'Well, I don't expect you to understand,' she conceded with a sleepy yawn. Her time clock had to be seriously skewed. 'Look, the fact is it's true that I didn't ever plan having sex before marriage, but that's not the reason I hadn't slept with Josh. I didn't sleep with Josh because I am really not his type.'

Emilio frowned skeptically. To his mind Megan was every man's type.

'I mean *really* not his type.'

Emilio stiffened. 'You're saying…?'

Megan nodded, amused by the look of amazement on his face. Propping her chin on her hands, she shook her head and teased, 'For a smart man you can be awfully slow sometimes.'

Emilio exhaled a long, slow breath. It whistled through his clenched teeth before he framed a grim smile, 'It certainly looks that way.'

'I really miss Josh.'

A few minutes ago this wistful statement would have roused Emilio to blind fury. Now he was able to offer a sympathetic smile and murmur, 'Gay?' Just to double-check the facts.

'Yes, my perfect flatmate was gay. He has gone to do aid work overseas. Josh is lovely. You'd really like him.'

She chattered on, blissfully unaware of the thoughts going through the head of the man beside her.

Gay! The guy he had spent a year being jealous of, twelve months torturing himself imagining the other man with Megan, and the guy was gay.

Did irony get any darker than that?

'Emilio?'

The questioning lilt in her voice roused him from his bitter reflections.

He rolled towards her.

'How did you know I shared a flat with Josh?'

'Philip must have mentioned it and I assumed.'

Rachel nodded. 'That must be it,' she agreed as she leaned across him, the tips of her breasts brushing his chest as she stroked his cheek. 'Wait until I tell Josh in my next letter.'

'Nobody writes letters,' he said, tangling his fingers in her hair.

'I do. There's something about putting a fountain pen to paper that's more personal,' she mused.

'Nobody saves themselves for their wedding night either.'

'Don't worry about it. I don't expect you to propose, Emilio. Marriage is not meant for men like you.'

She blinked in bewilderment as she found herself exiled from his arms. She turned her sleepy stare on Emilio, who was sitting upright in bed with his arms folded across his chest. He looked magnificent and inexplicably furious.

With a resigned sigh she pushed her hair back from her face and propped her chin on the heel of her hand. 'What's wrong?'

'What do you know about *men like me*? And what exactly would I be incapable of understanding?'

'Sorry, I didn't mean to generalise,' she soothed.

'But now you have—'

'I'm not judging,' she promised earnestly. 'And I'm sure you did love Rosanna, but you said yourself that being married didn't stop you from feeling sexually attracted to other women, and I'm sure most men are, but they don't act on it. You did.' The worst torture in the world, it seemed to Megan, would be to watch the man you loved cheat on you. 'You obviously tried not to be unfaithful.'

Emilio stared at her in amazement as she gave his shoulder a comforting pat.

'It's a fact of life that some men are simply not suited to monogamy or marriage.' She pushed away the sadness and added with a wicked laugh, 'But you do make the most perfect lovers.'

'We try,' Emilio husked, pulling her into his arms. 'We try. This time,' he promised, 'it will be better.'

'I don't see how,' Megan said honestly, though the idea of trying to achieve the impossible did hold its attractions.

He fitted his mouth to hers, one hand cupping her breast, the other stroking the smooth curve of her thigh.

'I'm going to touch you everywhere,' he whispered thickly. 'I'm going to taste all of you,' he told her as he slid his tongue between her parted lips. 'Everywhere,' he said, kissing her closed eyelids. 'All of you.'

Megan prised her eyelids open. She was breathing hard. 'You'll own me,' she whispered, thinking, You already do.

His dark eyes glowed with approval as he slid down her body. 'Believe it.'

Her entire body was bathed in a rosy glow of arousal as he parted her legs. Her heart thudded heavily as his hand slid between them, pushing them further apart, opening her up to him.

She gasped, her hips lifting from the bed at the first intimate touch.

'Relax. We're going to take our time, *querida*,' he soothed, stroking his tongue wetly along the silky skin of her inner thigh.

Megan closed her eyes and said, 'Oh, God, you're incredible.'

It was a theme she returned to on several occasions during the next couple of hours, because, true to his word, Emilio did take his time. He took her to the brink of paradise several times before he finally slid on top of her and led her screaming over the top into the waiting golden glow of fulfilment.

As they lay side by side, their bodies trembling and slick with sweat, he turned his head and grinned at her. 'I'd ask how it was for you but I think I already know. Who'd have guessed you were a screamer?'

'I'm just an excellent actress, that's all,' she teased, curling happily up to his side. 'Next time, Emilio, I wouldn't mind being the one driving you a little crazy.'

'Works for me. I have no problem at all with a woman in charge.'

It was a couple of hours later that Megan was woken by the sound of the door hitting the wall. She blinked to see Emilio approaching, bearing a tray.

He laid it on the bed.

'What's this?' she said, looking at the array of cold meats, cheese and crusty bread laid out.

Emilio pulled the cork on the bottle of red and filled two glasses. 'It's a picnic in bed.'

'I really don't have an eating disorder, you know.'

'You have expended a lot of energy.' Her blush made him grin. 'Any athlete will tell you that taking on fuel at regular intervals is essential to maintain performance.'

Glancing at the food, Megan realised without the prompting of her rumbling tummy that she was hungry. 'Shouldn't we get up? It's...' She glanced at the face of her watch and gasped. 'My God, we've been in bed all day.'

Emilio appeared unperturbed. 'Yes, deliciously decadent, isn't it? I could get used to it.'

I can't let myself, she thought.

Pushing away the sad thought and telling herself to just enjoy the moment, she sat up, pushing her hair from her face with both hands.

'I am quite hungry,' she admitted.

'I love watching you eat,' he said when she was allowing herself to be tempted by another piece of cheese. 'You do it with such...relish.'

'You mean I'm greedy.'

'So am I every time I look at you.'

'I feel so guilty.' She saw the flash of annoyance cross his face and added quickly, 'Not about the food or the sex, but it's a weekday and I haven't done a scrap of work. It's all right for you—you're your own boss.'

'Has it occurred to you that you could be too?'

She flashed him a surprised look. 'As a matter of fact, yes, it has.'

'You should. You're obviously not stretched now. You are capable of much more.' He hesitated. 'I know that your father might say that—'

'He'll hand the reins over to me?' she interrupted with a laugh. 'Oh, I know that's never going to happen. I'm a woman and I'm only accepted as an Armstrong up to a point, but I've learnt a lot working for him and made some very useful contacts.'

And he had been worried Armstrong was taking advantage of her. It turned out that Megan was no doormat. Emilio chuckled low in his throat.

'I'd ask you to come work for me, Megan, but it's a rule of mine not to mix business and pleasure.' With a low growl he lunged for her, rolling her underneath him. 'And you are definitely pleasure.'

CHAPTER FOURTEEN

MEGAN put down the gloss she was applying to her lips. She very much hoped to challenge, with a little bit of help from a tall Spaniard, the manufacturer's claim that it lasted for twenty-four hours, and fished her mobile from her open bag on the floor where it was ringing stridently.

She checked the caller identity and her brows lifted in surprise. She sat down on a linen hamper, telling herself not to assume the worst—it might not be bad news.

Though experience tended to suggest it would be. The last time her brother had rung he had lost his passport and all his money; the time before he'd rung from the casualty department, where he'd ended up after coming off his motorbike.

Unless in a scrape of some sort it was rare for her brother to return a call, let alone take the initiative. Typically, she thought, her smile becoming wry, he had chosen the worst time possible to make contact.

'Hi, Megan, and before you ask I'm fine.'

'I'm glad to hear it. Look, I'd like to chat, Phil, but this isn't actually a very good time,' she admitted, smiling to herself as she glanced towards the door, her stomach giving a little shimmy in anticipation as she thought of it opening any second to admit Emilio.

Her eyes half closed and her breath came a little faster

as an image of him standing in the doorway slid into her head. She was utterly powerless to control the response of her body to the mental image.

She had not seen him for three minutes tops and she already missed him. She smiled, recalling his response when she'd looked into the mirror and exclaimed, 'I look awful!' Privately she thought she looked pretty good for someone who had spent the best part of the day in bed.

'Is this where I'm supposed to say, no, you look fine?'

She pursed her lips and glared at his reflection in the mirror with feigned antagonism. 'Would it have hurt to tell a white lie?'

His glorious eyes smiled back at her. 'It wouldn't have been a white lie, *querida*, it would have been a massive lie.'

Megan struggled to adopt an indifferent expression. While she appreciated honesty as much as the next person, there was a time and a place and a limit to her new-found confidence.

'Because you don't look fine, you have never looked fine in your life. You are utterly breathtaking.' The carnal glow in his stunning eyes deepened as he elaborated on this theme in a voice that trickled over her like warm honey. 'Luscious, and incredibly sexy. The only flaw I can see is that you have too many clothes on,' he decided, flicking the collar of a blue chambray shirt she had appropriated from his wardrobe because, while she had become a shameless version of the Megan that awoke that morning, she was not as comfortable with the entire walking-around-naked thing as Emilio was.

It was possible nobody was as comfortable as him, she decided, unable even to glance at his tall, lean, perfectly sculpted body without feeling a heat prickle across the surface of her skin in response to the raw power and sheer animal grace he exuded. It helped slightly that he had pulled on a pair of silk boxer shorts.

He seemed massively amused when, in response to his accusation that she wasn't listening to him, she was driven to yell, 'What do you expect? I can't think while you're walking around like *that*!'

She discovered it was empowering to be told you looked sexy by a man who was the definition of the word.

But before she was able to enjoy the sensation and possibly tempt him to elaborate on the theme further he took charge and pulled her up from the dressing table stool where she sat. Grabbing her overnight bag from the floor, he dropped a hand on her slender shoulder and, ignoring her half-hearted protests—God, but she was putty in his hands—he steered her towards the room she sat in now.

A bathroom, but like none Megan had ever encountered, it was a marble-floored, decadently appointed space complete with a vast shower that had more gadgets than a space shuttle, and in centre stage, raised on a pedestal, was an enormous antique copper bath.

She was unable to repress an exclamation of admiration.

'You like, then?'

The way she saw it there was nothing not to like. 'My favourite room in the place.'

'I thought that was the bedroom.'

Megan tipped her head, intending to respond to his sly teasing remark, but was momentarily knocked off balance to discover, not the taunting amusement she had anticipated on his lean face, but a curiously intent expression.

'It's not the décor that made an impression in the bedroom.'

His heavy-lidded eyes darkened at the shy admission.

'While I don't think your looks can be improved on—'

the compliment made her flush with pleasure '—I could probably do with freshening up, though I admit I rather like the smell of you on my skin.'

She stared at him, her eyes enormous, quite shockingly aroused by his comment. 'I must smell of you too.'

'Then perhaps we should share the bath.'

Megan, her mind filled with the image of floating in that fabulous bath with him, hastily assured him that she had no strong objections to this idea. The fact was she had no objections to anything Emilio chose to do to her so long as it involved physical contact; she was already a total junkie for his touch.

Emilio excused himself, promising that the phone calls he needed to make to clear the rest of his day would only take a few minutes and suggesting she fill the tub in his absence.

The tub was filled and scented with some of the oils she had discovered, and she had been wondering whether to get into the water now or wait for Emilio to return when the phone rang, by which point she was leaning towards getting into the water, if only to see Emilio's reaction when he walked in. Though that would mean wasting the cute matching undies set she had already slipped on in the hope of having him take them off—it was a tough choice.

Tough choice? Strip or be undressed?

God, where was Megan Armstrong, the Megan Armstrong who barely knew how to flirt?

And who was the wanton hussy who had taken her place?

'Is Dad working you too hard?'

Megan, struggling to focus on what her brother was saying, gave a non-committal grunt.

'Silly question, of course he is,' her brother added, answering his own question, which suited Megan fine. If she could get away without telling an outright lie she would prefer to.

'Fine, I'll make it quick, you little workaholic.' He continued talking even faster than normal—which was very fast. 'I just had to ring, to say thank you. You really are a good sport.'

'I am?' Megan said, searching her memory for something she might have done recently that would deserve her brother's gratitude.

Nothing immediately sprang to mind. It was true she did intercede to smooth things over sometimes when hostilities flared up between Philip and their father. But things had been pretty peaceful lately. His son wearing a tie the last time he visited had put Charles Armstrong in a good mood for a month.

'I suppose it was Emilio's idea, and as usual,' he observed with an admiring chuckle, 'he was spot on the money.'

A bemused Megan shook her head, tensing at the name. 'You think so?' Her thoughts raced. How on earth did he know she was with Emilio?

'Oh, God, yes. It was a brilliant idea. I mean, if Rosanna knows he's with someone else whose name he actually knows she can move on with her life, hopefully in my direction.'

Megan's jaw dropped as she struggled to cope with the shocks that were coming thick and fast—Philip and Rosanna. Things were getting seriously *Twilight Zone*.

'Though you and Emilio!' He seemed unable to control his amusement any longer, and her brother's voice became suspended by laughter.

As she listened to Philip's incredulous laughter echoing down the line Megan sat there, the sick feeling in the pit of her stomach growing.

'I suppose it was a case of it's so crazy it must be true. I mean, it's not the sort of thing you'd make up unless you were a brilliant strategist like Emilio.'

'Oh, yeah, he's brilliant.'

Oblivious to the irony in her voice, Philip continued to congratulate her. 'Well, he had your help and however you pulled it off, little sister, I am very grateful. I suppose, when you think about it, you and Emilio wouldn't be any more crazy than me and Rosanna, but I love her, Megan, I really do.'

Megan closed her eyes and thought, God, I hope not! She really didn't want to see Philip get his heart broken. And if Emilio had decided he wanted his wife back that was inevitable. Emilio would let nothing stand in his way. Her brother had a great many excellent qualities; he was nice, but what woman, given the choice between nice and Emilio, was going to choose nice?

'I had no idea,' she said honestly. 'What I don't really understand is why you went to Emilio in the first place.'

'Other than habit, you mean.'

'You're not teenagers any more, Philip,' she said, a shade of irritation sliding into her voice.

'I suppose it does seem a bit weird, and I wasn't sure if I actually thought he could help, I just figured maybe if they talked… Closure and all that. But you know Emilio, he never lets you down, does he? Rosanna is totally convinced that you two are together and that's what matters. You must have put on quite an act. I wish I'd been there to see it.'

'You were about the only person that wasn't.'

'Well, don't tell Rosanna you noticed. According to her you two didn't have eyes for anyone but each other. In your own private world, she said,' he quoted. 'She also kept saying she didn't know why she was surprised, because when you thought about it it was obvious. Any idea what she meant?

'Not that it matters,' her brother continued. 'The thing is she can finally let go because she thinks you two are love's young dream. I think, Megan, that she's finally able to put her marriage behind her, now that she thinks Emilio is happy. Anyway, cheers, I'll let you know how things go. I'm just going to give Emilio a ring to say thanks.'

'I can save you the bother, Phil,' she said brightly. 'He's right here. Hold on a sec, I'll get him for you.'

Emilio had just finished filling the second champagne flute and was preparing to carry them into the bathroom with him when he heard the door open. He turned, glasses in hand, as Megan walked into the room, phone pressed to her ear.

His smile was not returned. A man did not have to be particularly intuitive to see that Megan was not happy. He wondered what had occurred in the few minutes they had been apart to account for her change of mood, but only in passing—his attention was focused on admiring how sinfully sexy she looked in a pink bra and a minuscule pair of matching silk shorts trimmed with lace.

His throat dry, his body hardening in lustful appreciation, he watched her advance, each angry step making her breasts jiggle gently under the silk.

Presumably she had not hated him when she had put on that outfit, unless she had intended to give him heart failure. Now she looked as though she would have preferred a more hands-on method of murder.

When she'd walked into the room the look she'd fixed him with was icily aloof, but by the time she had stalked across the room it had moved on to full-blown fury.

She paused about a foot short of him, still appearing to listen to the person speaking on the phone.

Emilio's lashes rested against the sharp angle of his jutting cheekbones as his heavy-lidded glance dropped down her smooth curves.

'You really do know how to make an entrance, *querida*,' he slurred admiringly.

Megan gritted her teeth. Even reminding herself that she hated him did not prevent her body responding of its own accord to his voice.

'Though if that's the outfit you were thinking of wearing for dinner, I think perhaps we should order in.'

Belatedly Megan realised that she had been so eager to confront him that she had forgotten what she was wearing, or, rather, what she wasn't!

She covered the mouthpiece with her hand. 'I'm not hungry,' she snapped, adding, just in case there were any doubts, 'For food, or you! And the only thing I need ordered is a taxi. Ask him yourself.'

Snarling the last disconnected remark in what he assumed was in response to what the person on the other end of the line was saying, she produced a saccharine-sweet smile and with no warning lobbed the phone at him—not gently.

Emilio managed to catch it in his free hand, only slopping a little champagne in the process.

'Well caught,' Megan admired, taking a glass. Holding his eyes, she took a deep swallow, then, wiping the moisture from her lips with the back of her hand, she made a sharp turn and walked stiff-backed towards the bathroom, resisting the temptation to run.

Just before she vanished inside she yelled over her shoulder, 'And stop staring at my bottom!'

Emilio chuckled throatily. 'Admit it, you'd be insulted

if I could.' His smile faded as she closed the door with a loud click.

There was zero chance of her being offended and zero chance of him letting Megan walk away. Eyes narrowed, he weighed the possibility of scaring her off by revealing his intentions. On balance he decided it was worth the risk. After two years of wasted time Emilio wasn't about to waste another minute.

He lifted the phone to his ear. 'Yes, Philip, I am here. Yes, she did say bottom.'

Five minutes later Emilio let himself into the bathroom.

Megan was standing at the mirror above the washbasin using some unladylike language as the slide she was trying to secure her hair with at the nape of her neck slithered along the silky strands onto the floor.

She picked it up and continued with her task, deciding to ignore his smouldering presence. A good idea in theory, but not actually easy to follow through with when the presence you were ignoring consisted of six feet five inches of solid bone, muscle and potent masculinity.

The sexual charge of his presence scorched its way across the room towards her. It would have been easier to ignore walking into a brick wall.

She was almost relieved when he broke the charged silence and spoke.

'At least you didn't lock the door.'

But she had unfortunately got dressed. He wondered if the pink things were still on underneath; he had every intention of finding out.

Megan slung him a dark look over her shoulder and was annoyed to see that he looked insultingly at ease with his broad shoulders propped casually against the wall. He didn't even have the decency to look defensive.

'Only because there isn't a lock.' Tongue caught between her teeth, her expression one of fierce determination, she finally managed to get the wretched slide to stay put.

With a little grunt of triumph she spun around chin high to face him, her expression a study of haughty disdain as she said, 'You could have knocked.'

The suggestion made him laugh. 'I think not.'

'Because the normal rules that govern society don't apply to Emilio Rios.'

Instead of responding to her sneering provocation, Emilio, a distracted expression in his dark eyes, produced a seemingly unconnected comment. 'The nape of your neck is very sexy—did you know that?'

Megan, hating herself for responding to the throaty comment, gave an indifferent sniff and lifted a protective hand to the area under discussion.

'We're not talking about my neck.' But he was still staring at it.

'I was.' He blinked and gave his head a shake as if to clear it. 'Look, I'm sorry to keep you waiting.'

'Don't flatter yourself,' she rebutted, her amber eyes flashing with antagonism. 'I wasn't waiting.'

Emilio acknowledged her cranky response with the sardonic elevation of one winged brow and continued as though she hadn't spoken. 'But explaining your presence to your brother required some—'

'Tact?'

'Patience.'

Of which Emilio had rapidly run out.

Rather than placating Philip, he had found himself delivering a few home truths. He had pointed out that the show of concern for his sister's welfare, as touching as it was, had kicked in pretty late in the day, and for the record he did not need to be told that Megan was not like the girls he normally dated. As for what she was doing in his apartment, he had left Philip in no doubt that it was none of his damned business.

'You should have mentioned I wasn't meant to tell him we had sex.'

His brows lifted. 'Did you?' he asked, sounding more interested than alarmed.

Megan picked up the hairbrush she'd just been using from the glass vanity unit above the basin and dropped it into her open holdall. 'It's not something I'm likely to boast about.'

The muscles around his angular jaw tightened, but she ignored the warning signs.

'I don't like to broadcast my mistakes. God knows why—'

'You slept with me? You gave me your innocence? We both know why, Megan.'

Megan's eyes fell from his. This was somewhere she could not go—not now, not if she wanted to cling to what shreds of dignity she retained.

'I doubt,' she muttered, 'Philip expected you to go as far as have sex with me to help him with his love life. God!' she exclaimed, her voice aching with disgust. 'Did this have *anything* to do with me?' she asked, banging her chest palm flat against her heaving chest.

'Oh, no, I was thinking about your brother the entire time we were making love,' he drawled. Shaking his head, he dragged a hand across his dark hair and ejaculated, *'Madre di Dios!'* He regarded her with an expression of utter incredulity. 'What are you talking about, woman?'

'I'm talking about spiking any chance Philip has with Rosanna and making Rosanna jealous.' She could see from his point of view it was a win-win situation.

'Leaving aside the why would I want either of these

things to happen, how exactly would sleeping with you achieve them?' Emilio levered his broad shoulders from the wall and took a step towards her, shrugging off his relaxed façade.

'It's glaringly obvious,' she contended.

Emilio was, Megan realised as their eyes connected in the mirror, pretty mad.

'Are you denying he asked you to intercede on his behalf with Rosanna?' Megan took a blind step backwards, reluctant to admit, even to herself, that she was daunted by the anger glinting in Emilio's eyes.

'Why would I deny anything? Are *you* denying you begged me to have sex with you?'

Megan compressed her lips and glared at him. 'It's always nice to be considered a charity case.'

'I've always considered you more of a challenge. By the way, Philip also extended an invitation to dinner. I refused on both our behalves.'

'I don't need you to do anything on my behalf!'

He adopted an expression of innocent enquiry as he countered, 'You wish to go to dinner with Rosanna and Philip?'

'He didn't really invite us, did he?'

'No.'

Megan gave a frustrated snort and spun away from him, causing her hair to break free again. With a sharp cry of frustration she dropped to her knees, but Emilio was faster than her; his long fingers closed around the errant item a second before she reached it.

Megan was unable to control her instinctive reaction as she pulled her hand back from his with the caution normally reserved for contact with white-hot metal.

Fully expecting him to make some sarcastic comment,

she was relieved but cautious when, squatting back on his heels, Emilio held his open palm out to her.

'Pretty,' he said, running the pad of his thumb over the antique tortoiseshell hair ornament.

Her relief evaporated when his dark lashes lifted from the razor-sharp angle of his high cheekbones. The expression in his deep-set dark eyes as he subjected her hair to an equally intense study sent a convulsive shudder up her spine.

Megan arranged her features in a prim expression, inhaling deeply to clear the fuzzy feeling in her head, and said, 'I like it.' Thinking, But not as much as I like your mouth.

The corners of his mouth curved upwards into a smile, but as his glance continued to move across the soft brown waves that surrounded her face it faded. 'But not as pretty as this.'

He stretched his hand towards her and every instinct of self-preservation she possessed screamed, Do not let him touch you!

But other, stronger instincts won out. They always would. Like it or not, the fact was he owned her body.

His long fingers barely brushed the skin of her forehead as he pushed a shiny strand from her eyes but the electric charge that zigzagged through her body felt like a lightning bolt.

'I prefer your hair loose,' he admitted, thinking of how it had looked spread out on the pillow around her flushed face. Thinking of burying his face in it, recalling the sensation of the silky strands brushing against his skin as she bent over his body.

Feeling his control slipping, Emilio banished the line of thought but could not resist touching her hair one more time.

Megan flinched away. 'Well, that's it, then,' she cried,

reaching out and snatching the hair slide from his open palm.

She rose jerkily to her feet and stared at it for a moment before slinging it wildly over her shoulder. She was close to tears and not sure who she blamed for this situation most—Emilio or herself.

So she hadn't known about Rosanna and Philip. She had known he'd kissed her at the airport for Rosanna's benefit, and she'd come with him anyway, knowing no matter how hard she had tried to pretend otherwise exactly where it was going.

But having it spelled out to her by Philip was a different matter. 'I will never tie my hair back again,' she declared, striving for ironic mockery and delivering instead something a lot closer to frenzied panic, possibly because the husky addition of, 'because I live to please you,' was uncomfortably close to the truth.

'Are you going to tell me what I've done to upset you?'

The quiet words sent a fresh flash of anger through Megan.

'Let me think…' she said, adopting a mystified expression as she pressed a finger to the suggestion of a cleft in her firm, rounded chin. 'Could it be something to do with the fact I don't much like being used? How do you think I felt having my brother thank me for playing along with your *brilliant* idea? He called me a good sport!'

His lips sketched a quick smile. 'Yes, that sounds like Philip.'

She searched his face. 'Don't you feel even slightly guilty?'

'What exactly should I feel guilty about, Megan?' His feral smile flashed, sexual and dangerous.

'You are utterly unbelievable!' she breathed, his indolent

pose incensing her further. The man was totally and completely shameless, she decided, shaking her head in disbelief. 'The fact that you can even ask that,' she said in a voice that quavered with anger.

'Philip thinks you're a great guy.' She shook her head, gave a bitter laugh and regarded Emilio in disgust.

Emilio folded his arms across his chest and studied her flushed, vivid little face, his expression softening as he watched her blink back tears from her glowing eyes.

Not for the first time he cursed the inconvenient timing of Philip's call. 'And you do not?'

'Me?' she said, sweeping the make-up she had used earlier to make herself look good for him into her open bag with her forearm.

'You do not think I'm a...*great guy*?'

She glared at him, felt the helpless longing roll through her and snarled, 'I think you're a selfish, manipulative rat!'

'Don't hold back now, say what you think,' he drawled with deceptive affability.

'Like you care what I think. You,' she accused, 'don't care what anyone thinks about you.'

It had been true.

It still was to a degree. The good opinion of others had never mattered to Emilio. He did not need people to love him.

He still didn't need people's approval or love—just one person's.

'But for the record I think you're cold, calculating and callous.'

His dark eyes glinted dangerously. 'Great alliteration,' he admired. 'But don't stop there when it's just getting interesting. How exactly am I...' he paused and selected an insult at random '...calculating?'

'You went to the airport to meet Rosanna.' Pretending to be Philip's friend and all the time intending to stab him in the back. 'And you kissed me!'

'True, but as I didn't know you would be there you can't really call my actions calculating. Now opportunistic…?' He shrugged his impressive shoulders, causing the powerful muscles in his chest to bunch beneath his satiny skin.

'You know exactly what I mean!' she snarled.

He directed a narrow-eyed considering look at her angry face.

The prolonged scrutiny began to make Megan feel uncomfortable and her scowl deepened in direct proportion to those feelings of discomfort. If I'm not careful, she reflected grimly, I'll be the one apologising!

Not that she expected for one minute that Emilio would apologise, but he could at least have the guts to acknowledge he'd done something wrong.

'I doubt very much if *you* know what you mean, but I have to say a pout actually looks pretty good on you.'

Her chest swelled wrathfully. 'I do not pout!'

His grin was deliberately provocative as he corrected his previous observation. 'Maybe not *pretty* good—make that very good.'

Megan sniffed and did not rise to the obvious bait as she regarded him coldly. 'It's bad enough you used me to make Rosanna jealous, but Philip doesn't have a clue you want her back, or at least don't want him to have her if you can't.'

'Have you ever thought of writing novels—I'm thinking fantasy here.'

Megan pointedly ignored his attempt to divert the conversation.

'He thinks you want him and Rosanna to be happy. He doesn't have the faintest idea about your hidden agenda.'

'And you think you do?'

Megan's last faint but persistent hope that she might have it wrong was extinguished when he didn't even attempt to deny her accusation.

'Yet despite that you are here with me.'

'That situation can change very quickly.' The retort, she knew, would have carried more weight if she had swept from the room.

So why aren't you?

'Philip is right. I would like to see Rosanna happy.' Whether the man to do this was Philip he was unsure. Emilio hoped so, but at that moment it was his own future happiness that dominated his thoughts and actions.

'And you think getting back with you would make her happy.'

'Being with me never made Rosanna happy.' And Emilio blamed himself for not realising it earlier. 'And that went doubly once she realised that I was in l—'

'Realised you were sleeping your way through the female population of Europe!' she interrupted shrilly.

A nerve clenched in his lean cheek before he flashed a quick sardonic smile as he drawled, '*Not* what I was about to say.'

Too angry to register the ironic inflection in his voice, Megan sneered. 'I suppose you're going to promise to be faithful to her.'

Emilio inhaled, his dark eyes flashing. 'You have finished?'

As she met his level stare Megan felt an irrational flicker of guilt. He was the one who should be feeling guilty, she reminded herself, and nothing she had said was not the truth.

CHAPTER FIFTEEN

'I WAS never unfaithful.'

'Sure you weren't…' Megan's voice died away as her eyes reconnected with Emilio's level stare. A flicker of confusion crossed her face that changed to astonishment as she gasped. 'You're serious!'

He dipped his head in curt acknowledgement.

'So if there weren't other women, why did you split up?'

Emilio studied her face for a long, thoughtful moment before he responded. Was it unreasonable, he wondered, to expect her to not think the worst of him, to allow for the possibility he might be the good guy, or at least attempting to be, just once?

'While I find it fascinating to be viewed as some sort of evil genius hatching diabolical plans and bending people to my will—' he drawled.

'Oh, no, you're one of life's innocents!' And he hadn't answered her question.

'No, Megan, that is you. Do you really imagine for one moment I kissed you at the airport because I wanted to make my ex-wife jealous, or help out your brother? I didn't plan on seeing you there any more than you planned to kiss me back. We did what we did because, *Dios*, do I have to spell it out? We have just spent the day in bed having the most incredible sex of my life!'

Clearly it was only a figure of speech, but even as she counselled herself not to take him too literally Megan had to snatch in a breath and grab the shelf beside her as her knees began to wobble, the excitement surging like a tide through her, and all the time painfully conscious of the excitement unfurling, hot and liquid, low in her pelvis.

'It may have been the *only* sex of your life,' he conceded, his lips twisting into a self-condemnatory smile—not only did he not regret this amazing discovery, he felt a knee-jerk rush of primal, possessive satisfaction as he thought about being Megan's first, her *only* lover.

Did that make him a total bastard?

'But you can't tell me that it—*I*—didn't move your world a little too.'

Megan stared back at him and shook her head mutely. She knew that today had changed her and her life for ever; she knew now what it was like to love a man, and even though Emilio wasn't talking about love he was right about one thing: her world had moved. Actually it had tilted on its axis.

His chin tilted to an arrogant, challenging angle. 'You can't look at me without wanting to rip off my clothes.' His liquid eyes darkened as they meshed with hers. 'You tremble when I touch you.'

It was clear from Emilio's expression that he was inviting her to respond, but Megan felt the words of denial locked in her emotionally congested throat. If she started speaking she was afraid she wouldn't be able to stop.

When it became clear she wasn't going to rise to the challenge he had thrown, Emilio sighed and dragged a hand down his strong shadowed jaw. 'You could meet me half-way. But fine…yes, I went to the airport with the intention of speaking to Rosanna, but I did not agree to act as a go-between for Philip. However,' he conceded, 'when we spoke yesterday I was concerned. I realised that he had a point. There were issues in our marriage that were perhaps not fully resolved.'

Megan, thinking, Like you being in love with her, did not bother to hide her scepticism. 'You didn't do much talking that I saw.'

'That is because I became distracted.' His eyes sought and found hers and the anger shining in the dark depths morphed into a potent blend of hunger and sensual appreciation.

Megan, who had no control over the tide of warm colour that washed over her skin, felt her stomach muscles flutter. Her helpless physical response to the sexual message in his eyes did not stop there. She was just glad that he could not see those other, more embarrassing physical responses.

'What distracted you?'

One corner of his mouth lifted, that crooked smile…it never failed to make her heart ache.

'You know the answer to that, Megan. And for the record you still are. You'll still be distracting me when I'm old enough to know better.'

The realisation did not appear to make him happy as, visibly leaking patience, he stalked with pantherlike grace to the other side of the room and slammed his hand against the wall before pressing his forehead to the cool tiles and breathing a heartfelt, 'Give me strength!'

After a moment he lifted his head, exhaling as his attention immediately switched back to Megan. As he read the expression on her face the furrow between his dark brows deepened.

The mixture of heady exhilaration and grim determination that had carried him through the day faded as he registered the wariness in her eyes. The idea that Megan could ever be afraid of him pierced him like a blade.

'I'm sorry...you...'

Megan didn't know what was more shocking: hearing Emilio say sorry or seeing him at a loss for words.

The natural hauteur in his manner was pronounced as he revealed abruptly, 'I am not accustomed to explaining myself.'

Her brows lifted. 'Imagine my amazement and, let me guess, you don't intend to start now.'

But it seemed he did intend to start.

'I do not want to resurrect my marriage, and Rosanna did not divorce me because I had been unfaithful. She divorced me because she knew I had fallen in love.'

The colour slowly seeped from Megan's face until even her lips were blenched white. The words, the last ones in the world she had imagined to hear coming from Emilio's lips, hung in the air between them.

She looked at Emilio, who had not moved an inch since he had made his shocking declaration. His lean face was shadowed, his expression unreadable; Emilio's dark lustrous stare remained trained on her pale face.

'You fell in love?' Why had this possibility never occurred to her?

His response echoed the sentiment. 'Is that so difficult to believe? You think I am not capable of feeling such things?'

Megan gave an awkward shrug. 'Of course not, no, I... just...' Her voice dried.

'It was not something I planned to happen. It was not actually something I believed possible. I felt in fact vastly superior to people who based their marriage on a temporary chemical imbalance, which in my mind equated to temporary insanity.' His lips twisted into a self-derisive smile as he admitted his previous arrogance with a disbelieving slight shake of his dark glossy head. 'I did not believe in something I could not see and taste and feel—then I did feel. I felt—' He stopped and swallowed, his bleak gaze sliding from hers.

Watching this man who had always appeared to be in charge of, not just himself, but everything else, display his vulnerability evoked a swell of empathy in Megan that was physically painful. She felt his struggle to rein in his emotions as deeply as she would have felt a blade sliding into her own heart.

The shocking realisation that he had had his heart broken was deeply disturbing on many levels, not least because she felt envious of the woman with whom Emilio had had the affair that had ultimately resulted in his marriage break-up.

Which left the question—why weren't they still together? Had the affair burnt itself out or was there another reason?

A reason that accounted for the haunted look in his dark eyes?

The nerve in his hollow cheek continued to clench and unclench. 'My feelings were not relevant—'

Not relevant, she thought, but evidently strong. 'Of course they were.'

'I was not free to act on them, because by that time I had already entered into a marriage of convenience.'

Megan braced her shoulders against the cool tiles of the wall; the alternative was falling down in a heap.

'Convenience? This is the twenty-first century. People don't— And anyway you and Rosanna were—' She stopped and lifted a shaky hand to her spinning head. 'God, I need a drink.'

Without a word he held his hand out.

For a moment Megan stared at it. Emilio waited, his expression hardening as she shook her head in a negative motion from side to side. Fighting to retain his upbeat mood in the face of her rejection, he was about to let it fall when she reached out and snatched at it, her small finger curling tightly around his.

Emilio had switched on a couple of lamps. The big room was illuminated by their soft glow that cast shadows across his face, emphasising the sheer perfection of his strong sculpted features.

The champagne in the glass she nursed had not lost its fizz. Megan dragged her eyes from his face and directed her gaze instead at the golden bubbles as she drew her knees up to her chin and took a deep gulp.

'Obviously it's none of my business.' She took a careful sip and looked at him over the rim of her glass. His response was a faint smile that told her nothing.

'And obviously you don't have to talk about it if you don't want to.'

He lifted a satirical brow and approached, bottle in hand.

'But you did bring up the subject,' she reminded him defensively.

'I did, didn't I?' Not at all in the manner he had intended, but he'd been reacting to events rather than anticipating them all day, and reacting in a way that was totally uncharacteristic.

Megan held a hand over her glass as he tilted the bottle.

She realised his glass was untouched, but then she could recall Philip once commenting during their college days that he'd never seen Emilio tipsy, let alone drunk!

'No, thank you.' The moment the well-mannered refusal left her lips the farcical quality of the scene hit her.

She bit down on her trembling lip to hold in the bubbles of laughter that welled in her throat.

'Care to share it?'

'I'm being served champagne by a man wearing silk boxer shorts who looks like—' Her glance swept from his toes to his glossy head, taking in all the perfect bits in between, and she felt her imagination go into overdrive and provide her with a slide show of seriously distracting images.

'Like?' he prompted.

Megan shifted her position, arranging her skirt modestly across her knees as she struggled to ignore the shameful liquid heat that flamed between her legs.

'Well, like you!' she burst out, frustration making her voice unattractively shrill.

In other words, perfect!

'Surreal does not even come close to describing all this. I feel like I've slipped into someone's fantasy.' She stared at his bronzed chest, watching the muscles glide beneath his satiny skin, and thought, Mine!

A glint appeared in his expressive eyes as he surveyed her flushed face. 'I could take offence at being treated like a sex object.'

'Which would be hypocritical considering the fact you enjoy flaunting your…your…'

'Almost as much as you enjoy looking, *querida*,' he taunted.

Megan, her cheeks burning, expelled a long shaky sigh as he vanished into the bedroom. A moment later he reappeared, zipping up a pair of faded jeans. His white shirt, which hung open, he made no attempt to fasten.

He held his hands wide. 'Better?' he asked, his gesture

inviting her opinion as he approached, his intention clearly to take the seat beside her on the vast sofa.

Megan breathed through a wave of paralysing lustful longing and experienced a moment's panic. 'We'll talk if you stay over there.'

'What,' he asked, looking torn between amusement and annoyance by her edict, 'are you talking about?'

'I'm talking about no touching.'

'No touching?' he echoed.

She shook her head. 'Touch me and I'm out of here.' Touch me and I'm toast. 'I know you think that all you have to do to close down any discussion is to kiss me, but—'

'Presumably, considering your rather elaborate precautions, I'd be right.'

Megan's amber eyes flew wide with indignation. 'That wasn't what I said—'

He arched a brow. 'No?'

Realising that was *exactly* what she'd been saying, she closed her mouth, wishing she could think of a smart line that would wipe that unbearably smug expression off his face.

'Naturally a man is always pleased to realise that he is actually irresistible.'

'Just stay over there, Emilio, please,' she begged, too weary to fight herself and him at the same time.

Their eyes held, for a moment she thought he was going to refuse, then he shrugged and turned, lowering his lean, rangy frame into a chair a few feet away.

He stretched his long legs out in front of him and, resting his chin on steepled fingers, arched an enquiring brow. 'Better?'

She nodded, thinking it wasn't better at all.

'You know, Megan, you can build as many walls as you like, I will—'

'Huff and puff and blow them down?'

He gave an appropriately wolfish grin. 'And leave myself open to the insult I am all hot air? No, I would remove your walls brick by brick, Megan.'

He didn't need to. With a cry she leapt up and flew across the room to him. She couldn't recall why she had put him at a distance, why they needed to talk—so she could hear more about some other woman? Was she out of her mind? She pressed her body to his, wrapping her arms around his neck.

'I don't want you not to touch me. I can't bear it,' she confided in an agonised whisper. 'Can I stay here tonight, with you?'

His slow smile was fierce and possessive, an emotion echoed in his kiss. 'What made you think that you were ever going anywhere?' he asked, sweeping her up into his arms.

CHAPTER SIXTEEN

MEGAN sat hunched forward, wrapped in a blanket of silent misery all the way to the airport. It seemed to take hours because, despite the hour, the early morning traffic was heavy and they got snarled up several times.

The taxi driver apologised in heavily accented broken English for the delays and reiterated his promise that he would get her to the airport on time to catch her flight.

Clearly misinterpreting the reason for his passenger's tension, he reeled off a list of statistics he had clearly memorised for such occasions that demonstrated flying was the safest form of transport.

Normally Megan would have tried to respond to his friendly overtures using her basic Spanish. It only seemed good manners to her to attempt to use the language when you were in a country. This time she didn't. She was afraid that if she opened her mouth she would start crying.

A hysterically weeping woman might not come under the heading of security threat, but she was not willing to take the gamble and risk being barred from the flight.

So she smiled and nodded instead and wondered again what Emilio would do when he woke up and found her gone.

Had he listened to his father's message?

She closed her eyes, hearing again the diatribe recorded on the answer machine.

The first half had been in Spanish, but as she had returned from the kitchen, her glass of water in hand, the speaker had slid unconsciously into English, a language he was equally fluent in, at least when it came to curses, which had liberally peppered his comments.

She had tried hard not to hear, even going so far as to hum softly to herself as she hurried through the room to drown out the sound of the voice she had identified as belonging to Luis Rios.

Emilio's father was clearly furious.

Then she had heard her father's name and stopped.

'Charles Armstrong was on to me half an hour ago. It turns out he gets the early edition of the damned British tabloids. Of course *he* was more than happy with the connection and shamelessly hinting at marriage plans—the man is deluded, but that is no reason to offend him. He can be useful to you and he does have influence in certain circles.

'What were you thinking of? You kiss the girl in an airport terminal packed with people with mobile phones, of course you end up on the front page. I've no doubt at all it will be all over the Internet. I can only hope there is nothing more incriminating out there.

'My son and a girl who is the daughter of some cleaner. *Por Dios*, what were you thinking of? If you're going to get involved with one of the Armstrong girls, did you have to make it the bastard? The other at least has some sort of pedigree. What have I told you? Bad blood will out! Well, I insist that it ends now. If not I will have no compunction in disinheriting you.'

The diatribe had continued, but by that point Megan had heard enough. She had dragged on her clothes, pausing only to take one last look at Emilio's sleeping face before she had left the building and hailed a cab.

Would he be angry or secretly relieved when he found she was gone and read her note?

She had her answer to the depressing question a lot sooner than she anticipated.

Having paid off the driver, she was walking towards the terminal building when a shadow fell across her. She automatically turned her head, just in time to see a tall figure clad in a black biker leather jacket remove his helmet.

'We cannot carry on meeting like this, *querida*.'

The sound of his soft accented drawl hit Megan with the impact of a thunderclap. Shock held her immobile. Totally paralysed, she gazed up blankly at the tall, rampantly male figure exuding masculinity from every pore and thought, He can't be here.

Logically he could not be here; she had left him sleeping. Was she hallucinating, or had she lost her mind?

Dragging a hand across his tousled dark hair, Emilio bared his teeth in a smile that left his dark eyes angry and cold as he stepped directly into her path, removing his designer shades as he did so, to pin her with a stare with the same penetrating quality as surgical steel.

People were staring, not because he was doing anything, just because he was Emilio—he was really here.

'You…here… I don't… How?' Megan stammered, barely able to hear her own voice above the pounding of her overstressed heart. 'Note… My note, it…' Frustrated by her inability to form a sentence, she stopped trying and lapsed into miserable silence.

Emilio arched a brow and took her arm, sliding the bag she carried from her shoulder. 'I always said if I ever found a woman who travels light I would not let her go.'

Her gaze made a slow journey up the long, lean length

of him. She released a fractured sighing gasp. He looked like a walking advert for mean, lean and dangerous—a leather-clad fallen angel.

'You have a motorbike?'

'It allows me more flexibility than a car does.'

Megan lifted a hand to her spinning head. 'I feel—not good.'

As he subjected her face to a searching, unsympathetic scrutiny Emilio felt his anger fall away and protective instincts rush in to fill the vacuum. She looked so incredibly fragile, the ribbons of soft colour along her cheekbones only accentuating her ghostly pallor, it physically hurt him to see her distress.

'You're not going to faint.'

Her outrage stirred in response to this typically heartless statement. 'Serve you right if I dropped dead at your feet.'

'That's more like it,' he approved, taking her elbow.

Megan, still in shock, responded to the pressure without thinking.

There was a time lag before she realised they were walking in the wrong direction. She directed a worried gaze up at his stern profile.

'My flight, it's…?'

Emilio carried on walking.

'Emilio.' She stopped dead. Short of dragging her, which she did not put past him, he would have to listen to her now.

He flashed an impatient look down at her before continuing to scan the rows of parked cars in the distance.

Watching him, Megan was conscious of details she had previously missed, like the pallor of his normally vibrant-toned olive skin and the lines of tension bracketing his mouth.

She pushed her disquiet aside, telling herself that all those things could be simply a result of sleep deprivation rather than anything more sinister, and goodness knew he had had very little last night. Cheeks flushed, she lowered her eyes and gritted her teeth as she forcibly expelled the erotic images from her head.

Better to worry about herself. If anyone was capable of looking after himself, it was Emilio.

'The car should be here,' he announced after consulting the metal-banded watch on his wrist.

She avoided the obvious question. 'Look, Emilio, I don't know how or why you're here but I left a note. I should be at check-in and—'

'I know you left a note.' A muscle clenched along his jaw. 'You have delightful manners, and excellent hand-writing, but neither are the reason I spent the last twenty-four hours in bed with you.'

The earthy disclosure sent a slam of desire through Megan's body. Lowering her eyes in the vain hope of dis-guising her reaction, she heard him say, 'I fully intended to spend the next twenty-four in much the same manner.'

This time there was absolutely no question of hiding her reaction.

She moaned a weak, 'Oh, God, Emilio!' And lifted her passion-glazed golden gaze to his. 'You can't say things like that to me.'

'Why?' He angled a satiric brow and smiled down into her face. 'It's true. Are you trying to tell me you don't want to go to bed with me?'

Megan flushed to the roots of her hair and cast an ago-nised look over her shoulder. Emilio had made no attempt to lower his voice and they were now attracting a great deal of attention.

'Will you lower your voice?' she hissed. 'People can

hear you.' And some enterprising person might snap a photo again.

Anger flashed across his face. 'Pity you cannot.' He might not have *said* the words, but he had told her in every other way possible that he loved her.

He had stripped his soul bare, broken the ingrained habit of a lifetime and lowered his defences to let her in, making himself vulnerable in the process.

She had frustrated his plans to make a formal declaration—a formality as far as he was concerned—by falling asleep in his arms after their last exhausting session of wild lovemaking.

To wake up and find her gone had been the low point of the last twenty-four emotionally turbulent hours. He had thrown on his clothes in a blind fury, fully intending when he picked up the ringing phone on his way to the door to slam it down.

Then he had heard his father's querulous voice saying, 'You haven't responded to my message.'

He had slammed the phone down then and listened to the message. What he heard confirmed his suspicions and explained pretty much why she had left, but where?

If in doubt it was Emilio's habit to follow his first instincts—he headed for the airport. He was confident that his motorbike and his knowledge of the city would considerably cut down on the journey time. The only problem being he had no idea how much of a head start Megan had on him.

He had actually been there less than five minutes before he saw her. His initial relief was followed by an equally intense rush of blind anger. How could she think that his father's threats meant anything to him? That he gave a damn who her mother was?

* * *

'Do I have to spell everything out for you?' he growled. 'Come,' he added, taking her elbow again, this time in a firm grip.

'My flight.'

He ignored her.

Megan struggled to inject a little common sense into the proceedings. 'Emilio, you can't kidnap me in broad daylight.'

'Kidnap implies coercion. You want to come with me,' he asserted confidently.

She bit her trembling lip and swallowed the lump of self-pity lodged in her throat. Was she destined to become one of those bitter people railing at the deal fate had dealt them?

She lifted her chin. 'A person cannot always have what they want.' Compared to others she had a lot: her health, friends, a good job.

But not Emilio!

Under the circumstances it was hard to feel suitably grateful.

Without warning Emilio halted, oblivious to the other people on the congested pavement. He cupped her chin in his hand and tilted her face up to him.

'But you want to stay with me?'

Emilio, a stranger to insecurity, despised himself for voicing the question, but he couldn't help himself.

The lie stayed locked in her throat. Instead Megan found herself nodding, her misted gaze missing the triumph that blazed bright in his eyes at her admission.

'It's been lovely.'

'Lovely?' Not the first word or even the last that sprang to his mind when he thought of the last twenty-four hours.

'I've really enjoyed myself, but duty calls. I have to

get back. Perhaps I could visit some time?' Oh, God, I'm babbling.

'On a friends-with-benefits basis?' He vented a hard laugh. 'Shall we check our diaries?' The mockery in his voice was savage as he shook his head and added, 'I think not, *querida.*'

'I didn't mean that. I meant…' She passed a hand across her eyes and admitted, 'I have no idea what I meant. Why did you have to come?' she wailed, past caring by this point if she attracted attention. 'Why couldn't you just let me go without a fuss?'

'I made that mistake once.'

Before she could question this cryptic statement or wonder about the odd, driven expression on his face, Emilio spotted what he had been looking for in the distance and changed direction.

'Come!'

Literally swept along, she had no time to think about resisting his imperious command; she was too busy trying to keep up with his long-legged pace.

She was panting by the time they reached the long, low, gleaming limousine.

'This is yours?'

He nodded.

'But what about your motorcycle?'

'It is hard to have a conversation while wearing a helmet.' He threw his own into the back seat and spoke to the uniformed driver who had emerged from the driver's seat when they appeared.

After exchanging words with Emilio in Spanish, he nodded courteously to Megan as he opened the rear passenger door and stood to one side.

Megan did not respond to the unspoken invitation. She

turned instead to Emilio, who stood there visibly oozing impatience at the delay.

'I don't want to talk to you.'

'I talk, you listen, whatever.'

Unprepared for his hands-on approach to the situation, Megan let out a soft shriek of protest as he scooped her up and placed her bodily inside the vehicle.

Ignoring both her shriek and the lucky punch she landed on his shoulder, Emilio slid in beside her and calmly indicated to the driver that they were ready to leave.

'I'm not ready!'

Her shrill protest went ignored by both men.

Megan smoothed down her skirt and turned in her seat to level a furious look at his impassive face.

'This is ludicrous. What do you hope to achieve by kidnapping me?'

'We have already established it is not kidnap, and as for what I hope to achieve—I suppose a degree of sanity.' His dark eyes skimmed her face as he sighed and admitted, 'It might be a long time before I let you out of my sight.' He would be afraid of closing his eyes for fear of her vanishing while he slept.

'Very funny.'

'I was not attempting to amuse you.'

'Has it occurred to you that someone might have snapped that little scene back there?' she asked him, nodding over her shoulder.

Emilio settled back in his seat and, taking advantage of the space offered by their luxurious transport, he stretched his long legs out in front of him and unzipped his leather jacket.

'Like yesterday morning, you mean.'

Megan stiffened, guilty colour flooding her pale face.

He knew she'd listened in and was probably furious about the invasion of his privacy.

'It wasn't deliberate. I didn't mean to listen to the message,' she told him earnestly. 'I was just going to get a drink of water when the answer machine kicked in. I was coming back to bed and then I heard Dad's name. I thought there might be a problem at home.'

Instead she had discovered that she was the problem.

'What an amazing relief. I thought for one awful moment that I was lumbered with the sort of woman who checks her man's emails and text messages.'

'I wouldn't— I—' Her wide indignant gaze flew to his face and she stopped. 'You're not serious.' Of course he wasn't serious—he'd called himself *her man*.

He gave a crooked smile. 'You think…?'

Her eyes fell from his. 'Have you spoken to your father? Is he still angry?'

'Probably.' He gave an uninterested shrug. 'My father is generally unhappy about something or other.'

Realising that he was downplaying the situation out of consideration for her feelings, Megan covered his hand with hers. 'It's all right, Emilio,' she soothed, producing a bright brittle smile to prove the point. 'It's nothing I haven't heard before.'

She stopped, a fractured sigh escaping her parted lips as he covered her hand, sandwiching it heavily between the two of his.

'It is something that you will not hear again!' he growled.

Ribbons of feverish colour appeared along her cheekbones as she gave a little laugh and stopped trying to tug her hand free. 'He's right, I am…a…b—'

Emilio cut across her in a voice that vibrated with outrage. 'Do not say it!'

Megan winced at the volume. 'All right,' she said, taken aback by the intensity of his response. 'But you have to remember your father is of a different generation. Things like that matter to him—'

'It is not a matter of age, it is a matter of ignorance. You will not make excuses for him.'

'All right,' she soothed. 'I won't. Can I have my hand back?'

'No.'

His brooding expression as he stared at her intensified the dark fallen-angel look and made her hopelessly receptive heart skip several beats.

'You will ignore anything you heard my father say,' he instructed grimly. There was menace in his expression as he scanned her face, exuding offended masculine aggression. 'How dare he?'

It was becoming clear to Megan that this was more about Emilio's relationship with his father than her. She wondered how the older man could not realise that issuing edicts to a man like Emilio was the equivalent of waving a red rag to a bull!

Emilio was the sort of person who would not give an inch if pushed, even if it was against his best interests. He was just too stubborn for his own good.

'I thought you might react this way. That's why I left.'

He arched an interrogative brow. 'What way would that be?'

He had no idea what was going on in her head, but he seriously doubted that she was about to say, You were blind to everything except the compelling need to find me and bind me to you.

She didn't.

'Admit it, Emilio, if you hadn't been determined to prove to your father that he has no control over you, you wouldn't have hared off after me this way. But, point proved—do you think you could take me back to the airport?'

Emilio vented a harsh laugh and dragged a hand through his hair. 'The way your mind works is a continual source of fascination to me.' Not to mention frustration. 'So if we follow your logic, if my father had told me to marry you I would have shown you the door to prove a point?'

'I'm not saying you'd go that far, but—' She stopped, her throat drying as he leaned in towards her.

His eyes were trained on her mouth as he said softly, 'I think you will find that there is no limit to how far I would go to protect what is mine.'

'You don't think your father would really disinherit you, would he?'

A sound of frustrated incredulity whistled through his clenched white teeth as he drew back. 'I am not talking about money! My father's threats mean nothing to me. He said he would disinherit me when I got divorced and my response was then what it would be now—I said, "Fine, go ahead."'

'You called his bluff.' A risky policy, but then Emilio was a born risk taker.

'Blackmail only works if you care about the thing that is being threatened.' His broad shoulders lifted in a shrug. 'I enjoy what I do, and I'm good at it, but if it vanished tomorrow and I had to start again I would not lose any sleep. My father, however, who is enjoying his retirement, has some very expensive hobbies—I am very good at making money and he enjoys spending it.'

'So he wouldn't disinherit you.' Megan gave a sigh. 'Well, thank God for that, but if necessary I'll speak to him myself and explain there's no chance of us…you know, of me polluting the Rios gene pool or anything.'

Aware that her laugh had a hollow, unconvincing sound,

she struggled to inject more conviction into her voice as she added, 'That it was just, you know…'

'No, I do not *you know*. Perhaps you would like to tell me *you know*.'

'Just sex, casual sex.' She saw anger flame hot in his eyes and, lifting her chin to a defiant angle, cried, 'What… what have I said now?'

A pulsing silence followed her question.

Emilio struggled to speak past the knot of anger lodged in his chest. 'I know about just sex. I have had just sex, you have not.'

'Great sex, then,' she admitted in a small voice.

A muscle clenched along his jaw. 'We made love, Megan.'

She felt his hand tighten over hers until it hurt, but she barely registered the pain. She couldn't take her eyes off his face and the impossible, incredible things she was seeing in his eyes.

'I've dreamt about making love to you for two years.'

Megan's stomach took a lurching dive. She stared at him, her head spinning. She was feverishly shaking—literally shaking from head to toe in reaction to this amazing statement.

He lifted the hand under his and, still holding her eyes, raised it to his lips. 'But the reality, *mi esposa*, was much, much better than dreams.'

The throaty confession sent a shudder through her body.

'Emilio…I don't understand…' I'm the one dreaming, she thought, not allowing herself to believe the possessive, tender glow in his eyes meant what she wanted it to mean.

'Do you think I don't know that?' He groaned. 'You are without exception the most clueless woman it has ever been my misfortune to fall in love with.' He stared into her face, drinking in the beauty of her delicate features like a starving man. 'Actually, the only woman I have ever fallen in love with.'

She started to shake her head. That was wrong; she knew that was wrong. 'But you loved… You still love… the woman who—'

'You still don't get it, do you?' He framed her face in his big hands. 'I fell in love with you, Megan. You are that woman.' The relief of having finally told her after two years' delay sent a rush of adrenaline through his body.

The low hum of confusion in her head had become a loud buzz. Megan, hardly daring to move, slowly lifted her wary gaze to his face. He was totally still, not an eye-lash flickered, not a muscle moved as, deathly pale, he looked back at her with eyes that glittered with a febrile intensity.

'Me?' Was this a joke? If so it was in the worst possible taste. 'But you left your wife, you—' She stopped, the moment of comprehension causing the blood to slowly seep from her face until she was parchment pale. 'That was me?'

'*Is* you,' he corrected huskily. 'Why is that so hard for you to believe?'

He dabbed his thumb to the tear running unchecked down her cheek, his smile so tender that more tears welled in her eyes. Her heart felt full enough to explode.

'But you didn't like me.'

Her protest was lost in his long, lingering, tender kiss.

Finally Emilio lifted his head, but only fractionally. He stayed close, close enough for their breaths to mingle as they stared in silence at one another.

If I'm dreaming, Megan thought, I definitely don't want to wake up.

She slid her hands under his leather jacket, pulling herself closer as she pressed her hands flat against his chest, feeling the warmth of his skin through the cotton of the T-shirt he wore underneath, feeling the heavy, strong, hypnotic thud of his heart through her fingertips.

'You feel real.' He felt marvellous.

Emilio smiled and nipped gently at the full curve of her lower lip with his teeth.

'And you feel delicious,' he said, sliding a hand under her skirt and along the smooth, silky skin of her outer thigh. Megan caught her breath sharply. 'You have the most incredible skin.'

Megan felt regret when he removed his hand. If he had decided to make love to her in the back of this limo with only a tinted-glass panel separating them from the driver it would not have crossed her mind to stop him. She would have gone out of her way to assist him!

The realisation came with not a scrap of shame.

'But, Emilio,' she said, frowning as she struggled to sort out the puzzles and unanswered questions in her head, 'I don't… How… That weekend.'

'That weekend,' he said heavily.

'You snubbed me. You barely spoke to me and then you told me I was a tart!'

'That weekend I *couldn't* look at you.' Dark colour stained his cheekbones as he forced himself to meet her gaze now. *'Por Dios,'* he groaned, pulling back from her, his face dark with the remembered pain as he dragged not quite steady hands over his sleek dark hair.

'I couldn't even trust myself to be in the same room as you for fear of giving myself away! To make it worse I *knew* that you were attracted to me.'

'I knew it!' she cried, leaning back in her seat and clapping a hand to her forehead, feeling utterly mortified in retrospect. 'I knew you knew. It was awful—you made me feel so…so… When I sat next to you at dinner that first night I couldn't breathe… I really thought I was having a panic attack or something. There were freesias on the window sill—I can't smell a freesia now without hyperventilating!'

'I do not remember flowers, but I do remember you arriving late during dinner looking so…' Sucking in air through flared nostrils, he sighed and shook his head. 'It was as if I was seeing you for the first time. You took my breath away.

'But I fought it. I was not willing to admit even then that such a thing was possible. Love was a fantasy, my life was planned, my work, a wife who made no emotional demands on me. Emotional detachment makes life easy, but I didn't realise until that night how lonely it can make you too.'

Moved beyond tears by the husky confession, she reached up and touched his cheek lovingly. For this strong, self-contained man to acknowledge, let alone confess, any weakness must, she knew, have taken great courage.

'And when I caught that loser in the car with you I knew, *I knew*, and I wanted you so much that not touching you was like some sort of— It was sheer torture. It—'

He stopped, his startled expression morphing into one of desire as Megan grabbed his face between her hands and pulled him towards her.

Nose resting against his, she closed her eyes and breathed in his warm male smell, then fitted her mouth to his. For a split second he did not respond to the pressure of her lips, then with a groan he kissed her back with a fierce hunger and bruising urgency that awoke an equal hunger in her.

'Wow!' She breathed in shakily when they drew apart.

'Indeed…wow!' Emilio echoed, looking almost as shaken as she felt.

Megan turned her head and kissed the hand pressed to her cheek before she held it there. 'Why didn't you touch me, Emilio?'

'I was married.'

'Of course.' She blushed that she needed reminding—reminding that Emilio was a man of honour and finding himself in such a situation must have been incredibly difficult. 'But afterwards, when you were divorced, why on earth didn't you…?'

He arched a brow.

'Come and get me,' she said simply.

'I did,' he admitted. 'After a decent interval passed—the last thing I wanted was anyone calling you the other woman—I came to your flat intending to sweep you off your feet and into my bed.' One corner of his mouth curled upwards into a self-derisive smile. 'It never even crossed my mind that you would not be there waiting for me.

'So I was not prepared for your door to be answered by a half-naked man of more than average good looks who informed me you were in the shower.'

'Josh!' she exclaimed.

He nodded. 'Your gay flatmate, yes, I know this now, but at the time I jumped to the obvious conclusion,' he admitted. 'It is never pleasant to feel a fool or have your heart and hopes crushed.

'I felt—' His apologetic glance swept across her face. 'It was totally irrational, I know, but in my mind you had betrayed me. My pride would not allow me to follow my instincts and take you from this man. I told myself you would do the running the next time. Deep down I think I never lost hope there would be a next time.

'Then when Philip let slip that your lover, or so I thought, had moved out, I felt... Let's just say I was not unhappy for your loss. The next day I went to the airport to assure Rosanna that there was no need to feel bad that things hadn't worked out for me with the woman she knew I had not pursued because we were still married. I spent the journey to the airport thinking of you and suddenly there you were. I was not thinking about Rosanna or anything when I kissed you.

'I just followed my instincts. If only I had followed my baser instincts when your friend opened the door that day the last year might have been very different.'

The pain and self-recrimination on his face made her tender heart ache. 'I was jealous of all the skinny, beautiful women I saw you photographed with,' she confessed. 'And no matter how hard I dieted I never looked like them.'

'*Por Dios!*' he ejaculated, looking horrified. 'I would never want you to look like those women. I love your curves. It is as a woman should be—warm and soft. And you will never diet again,' he announced firmly.

His vehemence made her smile. Her smile faded as she looked into the face she adored and declared with husky sincerity, 'I really do love you, Emilio.' Her golden eyes glowed as she ran a loving finger over the roughened curve of his cheek.

'And I love you.'

The kissing lasted until they drew up outside the building that housed Emilio's temporary accommodation. Neither occupant of the back seat noticed the car had stopped and the discreet driver made no attempt to announce the fact.

Megan laid her head on his chest and sighed with pleasure. 'And the good thing is when I leave the firm and set up on my own I'll be able to come to Madrid a lot more often, and maybe you will be able to come over to London occasionally too?'

She angled a look of tentative enquiry at his face.

'But surely you will set up your business here? In the short term I can help you with any language problems, though obviously enrolling on an intensive language course would be the obvious course of action.'

'You want me to move here… Are you asking me to move in with you, Emilio?'

He shook his head. 'I am asking you to marry me, *mi esposa*. I thought that was a given.'

Megan gasped. 'Not to me.'

'You wish time to think about it?' He glanced at his watch. 'Will three seconds suffice?'

Megan's expression of solemn shock melted into laughter as he delivered his outrageous offer.

'It will have to suffice, *querida*, because I have been waiting for your answer for two years and every extra second is taking a year off my life.'

He was right; the knowledge made her relax. Why stress over a choice she had already made?

'Well, I wouldn't want that because I want my husband to be around for a very, very long time.'

Emilio released the breath he had been holding—holding, it seemed to him, for two years. 'You will not regret this. I promise you, Megan, that you will not regret this,' he cried, pulling her to him and raining kisses on her upturned features. Finally he found her mouth and the last long, languid, achingly tender kiss lasted a very long time.

It was Megan who pulled out of his arms with a laugh. 'I have just realized—not when you were kissing me, obviously.' There was no room for anything but Emilio in her head when he kissed her. 'How long have we been here—not in the car, in Madrid?'

Emilio consulted his watch. 'Almost twenty-four hours exactly.'

'Do you realise I have been in one of the most vibrant, colourful cities in the world for twenty-four hours and all I've seen of it is the airport and your apartment? God, we've arrived back and I hadn't even realised.'

'That is indeed truly shocking!' Emilio agreed, tongue firmly in cheek. 'I feel I should share more shocking news. I do not have sightseeing trips planned for the immediate future.'

Her lips twitched as she adopted an innocent expression. 'What do you have planned?'

A wicked smile that made her pulse race split his dark features. 'Come with me, *mi querida*, and I will show you.'

Megan grinned back and took the hand he offered. This was one offer she had no intention of refusing. 'Why not? Madrid will still be here tomorrow.'

'Also next week.' The teasing smile faded from his handsome face as he took her hands in his. 'And so will I. I will always be here for you, Megan.'

The simple statement meant more to Megan than the vows they would soon exchange with equal solemnity. She nodded and said in a clear voice that shook with the depth of the emotions she wanted to convey, 'And I will always be there for you Emilio.'

Tears of emotion glowed in her eyes as Megan allowed him to lead her out into the morning sun and her new life.

Coming Next Month

from **Harlequin Presents®**. Available July 26, 2011.

#3005 THE MARRIAGE BETRAYAL
Lynne Graham
The Volakis Vow

#3006 THE DISGRACED PLAYBOY
Caitlin Crews
The Notorious Wolfes

#3007 A DARK SICILIAN SECRET
Jane Porter

#3008 THE MATCHMAKER BRIDE
Kate Hewitt
The Powerful and the Pure

#3009 THE UNTAMED ARGENTINEAN
Susan Stephens

#3010 PRINCE OF SCANDAL
Annie West

Coming Next Month

from **Harlequin Presents® EXTRA**. Available August 9, 2011.

#161 REPUTATION IN TATTERS
Maggie Cox
Rescued by the Rich Man

#162 THE IMPOVERISHED PRINCESS
Robyn Donald
Rescued by the Rich Man

#163 THE MAN SHE LOVES TO HATE
Kelly Hunter
Dirty Filthy Money

#164 THE PRIVILEGED AND THE DAMNED
Kimberly Lang
Dirty Filthy Money

Visit www.HarlequinInsideRomance.com
for more information on upcoming titles!

REQUEST YOUR FREE BOOKS!

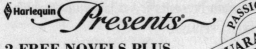 

2 FREE NOVELS PLUS
2 FREE GIFTS!

YES! Please send me 2 FREE Harlequin Presents® novels and my 2 FREE gifts (gifts are worth about $10). After receiving them, if I don't wish to receive any more books, I can return the shipping statement marked "cancel." If I don't cancel, I will receive 6 brand-new novels every month and be billed just $4.05 per book in the U.S. or $4.74 per book in Canada. That's a saving of at least 15% off the cover price! It's quite a bargain! Shipping and handling is just 50¢ per book in the U.S. and 75¢ per book in Canada.* I understand that accepting the 2 free books and gifts places me under no obligation to buy anything. I can always return a shipment and cancel at any time. Even if I never buy another book, the two free books and gifts are mine to keep forever.   106/306 HDN FC55

Name	(PLEASE PRINT)

Address	Apt. #

City	State/Prov.	Zip/Postal Code

Signature (if under 18, a parent or guardian must sign)

Mail to the **Reader Service:**
IN U.S.A.: P.O. Box 1867, Buffalo, NY 14240-1867
IN CANADA: P.O. Box 609, Fort Erie, Ontario L2A 5X3

Not valid for current subscribers to Harlequin Presents books.

**Are you a current subscriber to Harlequin Presents books
and want to receive the larger-print edition?
Call 1-800-873-8635 or visit www.ReaderService.com.**

* Terms and prices subject to change without notice. Prices do not include applicable taxes. Sales tax applicable in N.Y. Canadian residents will be charged applicable taxes. Offer not valid in Quebec. This offer is limited to one order per household. All orders subject to credit approval. Credit or debit balances in a customer's account(s) may be offset by any other outstanding balance owed by or to the customer. Please allow 4 to 6 weeks for delivery. Offer available while quantities last.

Your Privacy—The Reader Service is committed to protecting your privacy. Our Privacy Policy is available online at www.ReaderService.com or upon request from the Reader Service.

We make a portion of our mailing list available to reputable third parties that offer products we believe may interest you. If you prefer that we not exchange your name with third parties, or if you wish to clarify or modify your communication preferences, please visit us at www.ReaderService.com/consumerschoice or write to us at Reader Service Preference Service, P.O. Box 9062, Buffalo, NY 14269. Include your complete name and address.

*Once bitten, twice shy. That's Gabby Wade's motto—
especially when it comes to Adamson men.
And the moment she meets Jon Adamson her theory
is confirmed. But with each encounter a little something
sparks between them, making her wonder if she's been
too hasty to dismiss this one!*

*Enjoy this sneak peek from ONE GOOD REASON
by Sarah Mayberry, available August 2011
from Harlequin® Supperromance®.*

Gabby Wade's heartbeat thumped in her ears as she marched to her office. She wanted to pretend it was because of her brisk pace returning from the file room, but she wasn't that good a liar.

Her heart was beating like a tom-tom because Jon Adamson had touched her. In a very male, very possessive way. She could still feel the heat of his big hand burning through the seat of her khakis as he'd steadied her on the ladder.

It had taken every ounce of self-control to tell him to unhand her. What she'd really wanted was to grab him by his shirt and, well, explore all those urges his touch had instantly brought to life.

While she might not like him, she was wise enough to understand that it wasn't always about liking the other person. Sometimes it was about pure animal attraction.

Refusing to think about it, she turned to work. When she'd typed in the wrong figures three times, Gabby admitted she was too tired and too distracted. Time to call it a day.

As she was leaving, she spied Jon at his workbench in the shop. His head was propped on his hand as he studied blueprints. It wasn't until she got closer that she saw his eyes were shut.

He looked oddly boyish. There was something innocent and unguarded in his expression. She felt a weakening in her resistance to him.

"Jon." She put her hand on his shoulder, intending to shake him awake. Instead, it rested there like a caress.

His eyes snapped open.

"You were asleep."

"No, I was, uh, visualizing something on this design." He gestured to the blueprint in front of him then rubbed his eyes.

That gesture dealt a bigger blow to her resistance. She realized it wasn't only animal attraction pulling them together. She took a step backward as if to get away from the knowledge.

She cleared her throat. "I'm heading off now."

He gave her a smile, and she could see his exhaustion.

"Yeah, I should, too." He stood and stretched. The hem of his T-shirt rose as he arched his back and she caught a flash of hard male belly. She looked away, but it was too late. Her mind had committed the image to permanent memory.

And suddenly she knew, for good or bad, she'd never look at Jon the same way again.

Find out what happens next in ONE GOOD REASON, available August 2011 from Harlequin® Superromance®!

Celebrating

Blaze **10** *years of* red-hot reads

Featuring a special August author lineup of
six fan-favorite authors who have written
for Blaze™ from the beginning!

The Original Sexy Six:

Vicki Lewis Thompson
Tori Carrington
Kimberly Raye
Debbi Rawlins
Julie Leto
Jo Leigh

Pick up all six Blaze™
Special Collectors' Edition titles!

August 2011

Harlequin _Presents_

USA TODAY *bestselling author*

Lynne Graham

introduces her new Epic Duet

THE VOLAKIS VOW
A marriage made of secrets…

Tally Spencer, an ordinary girl with no experience of relationships… Sander Volakis, an impossibly rich and handsome Greek entrepreneur. Sander is expecting to love her and leave her, but for Tally this is love at first sight. Little does he know that Tally is expecting his baby…and blackmailing him to marry her!

PART ONE:
THE MARRIAGE BETRAYAL
Available August 2011

PART TWO:
BRIDE FOR REAL
Available September 2011

Available only from Harlequin Presents®.